THE CRYSTAL WORLD

by the same author

THE DROWNED WORLD
THE VOICES OF TIME
THE TERMINAL BEACH
THE DROUGHT
THE CRYSTAL WORLD
THE DAY OF FOREVER
THE VENUS HUNTERS
THE DISASTER AREA
THE ATROCITY EXHIBITION
VERMILION SANDS
CRASH
CONCRETE ISLAND
HIGH-RISE
LOW-FLYING AIRCRAFT
THE UNLIMITED DREAM COMPANY
HELLO AMERICA
MYTHS OF THE NEAR FUTURE
EMPIRE OF THE SUN
THE DAY OF CREATION

The Crystal World

J. G. Ballard

FARRAR, STRAUS & GIROUX
NEW YORK

*By day fantastic birds flew through the petrified forest,
and jeweled crocodiles glittered like heraldic salamanders
on the banks of the crystalline river. By night the illuminated man raced among the trees, his arms like golden
cartwheels, his head like a spectral crown . . .*

Contents

I Equinox

II The illuminated man

I

Equinox

The
dark
river

Above all, the darkness of the river was what impressed Dr. Sanders as he looked out for the first time across the open mouth of the Matarre estuary. After many delays, the small passenger steamer was at last approaching the line of jetties, but although it was ten o'clock the surface of the water was still gray and sluggish, leaching away the somber tinctures of the collapsing vegetation along the banks.

At intervals, when the sky was overcast, the water was almost black, like putrescent dye. By contrast, the straggle of warehouses and small hotels that constituted Port Matarre gleamed across the dark swells with a spectral brightness, as if lit less by solar light than by some interior lantern, like the pavilions of an abandoned necropolis built out on a series of piers from the edges of the jungle.

This pervading auroral gloom, broken by sudden inward shifts of light, Dr. Sanders had noticed during his long wait at the rail of the passenger deck. For two hours the steamer had sat out in the center of the estuary, now and then blowing its whistle at the shore in a half-hearted way. But for the vague sense of uncertainty induced by the darkness over the river, the few passengers would have been driven mad with annoyance. Apart from a French military landing craft, there seemed to be no other vessels of any size berthed along the jetties. As he watched the shore, Dr. Sanders was almost certain that the steamer was being deliberately held off, though the reason was hard to see. The steamer was the regular packet boat from Libreville, with its weekly cargo of mail, brandy and automobile spare parts, not to be postponed for more than a moment by anything less than an outbreak of the plague.

Politically, this isolated corner of the Cameroon Republic was still recovering from an abortive coup ten years earlier, when a handful of rebels had seized the emerald and diamond mines at Mont Royal, fifty miles up the Matarre River. Despite the presence of the landing craft—a French military mission supervised the training of the local troops—life in the nondescript port at the river mouth seemed entirely normal. Watched by a group of children, a jeep was at that moment being unloaded. People wandered along the wharves and through the arcades in the main street, and a few outriggers loaded with jars of crude palm oil drifted past on the dark water toward the native market to the west of the port.

Nevertheless, the sense of unease persisted. Puzzled by the dim light, Dr. Sanders turned his attention to the inshore areas, following the river as it made a slow clockwise turn to the southeast. Here and there a break in the forest canopy marked the progress of a road, but otherwise the jungle stretched in a flat olive-green mantle toward the inland hills. Usually the forest roof would have been bleached to a pale yellow by the sun, but even five miles inland Dr. Sanders could see the dark green arbors towering into the dull air like immense cypresses, somber and motionless, touched only by faint gleams of light.

Someone drummed impatiently at the rail, sending a stir down its length, and the half-dozen passengers on either side of Dr. Sanders shuffled and muttered to one another, glancing up at the wheelhouse, where the captain gazed absently at the jetty, apparently unperturbed by the delay.

Dr. Sanders turned to Father Balthus, who was standing a few feet away on his left. "The light—have you noticed it? Is there an eclipse expected? The sun seems unable to make up its mind."

The priest was smoking steadily, his long fingers drawing the cigarette half an inch from his mouth after each inhalation. Like Sanders, he was gazing, not at the harbor, but at the forest slopes far inland. In the dull light his thin scholar's face seemed tired and fleshless. During the three-day journey from Libreville he had kept to himself, evidently distracted by some private matter, and only began to talk to his table companion when he learned of Dr. Sanders's post at the Fort Isabelle leper hospital. Sanders gathered that he was returning to his parish at Mont Royal after a sabbatical month, but there seemed something a little too plausible about this explanation, which he repeated several times in the same automatic phrasing, unlike his usual hesitant stutter. However, Sanders was well aware of the dangers of imputing his own ambiguous motives for coming to Port Matarre to those around him.

Even so, at first Dr. Sanders had suspected that Father Balthus might not be a priest at all. The self-immersed eyes and pale neurasthenic hands bore all the signatures of the impostor, perhaps an expelled novice still hoping to find some kind of salvation within a borrowed soutane. However, Father Balthus was entirely genuine, whatever that term meant and whatever its limits. The first officer, the steward and several of the passengers recognized him, complimented him on his return and generally seemed to accept his isolated manner.

"An eclipse?" Father Balthus flicked his cigarette stub into the dark water below. The steamer was now overrunning its own wake, and the veins of foam sank down through the deeps like threads of luminous spittle. "I think not, Doctor. Surely the maximum duration would be eight minutes?"

In the sudden flares of light over the water, reflected off the sharp points of his cheeks and jaw, a harder profile for a moment showed itself. Conscious of Sanders's critical eye, Father Balthus added as an afterthought, to reassure the doctor: "The light at Port Matarre is always like this, very heavy and penumbral— do you know Böcklin's painting, 'Island of the Dead,' where the cypresses stand guard above a cliff pierced by a hypogeum, while a storm hovers over the sea? It's in the Kunstmuseum in my native Basel—" He broke off as the steamer's engines drummed into life. "We're moving. At last."

"Thank God for that. You should have warned me, Balthus."

Dr. Sanders took his cigarette case from his pocket, but the priest had already palmed a fresh cigarette into his cupped hand with the deftness of a conjurer. Balthus pointed with it to the jetty, where a substantial reception committee of gendarmerie and customs officials was waiting for the steamer. "Now, what nonsense is this?"

Dr. Sanders watched the shore. Whatever Balthus's private difficulties, the priest's lack of charity irritated him. Half to himself, Sanders said dryly: "Perhaps there's a question of credentials."

"Not mine, Doctor." Father Balthus turned a sharp downward glance upon Sanders. "And I'm certain your own are in order."

The other passengers were leaving the rail and going below to collect their baggage. With a smile at Balthus, Dr. Sanders excused himself and began to make his way down to his cabin. Dismissing the priest from his mind—within half an hour they would have disappeared their separate ways into the forest and whatever awaited them there—Sanders felt in his pocket for his passport, reminding himself not to leave it in his cabin. The desire to travel incognito, with all its advantages, might well reveal itself in some unexpected way.

As Dr. Sanders reached the companionway behind the funnelhouse, he could see down into the afterdeck, where the steerage passengers were pulling together their bundles and cheap suitcases. In the center of the deck, partly swathed in a canvas awning, was a large red-and-yellow-hulled speedboat, part of the cargo consignment for Port Matarre.

Taking his ease on the wide bench seat behind the steering helm, one arm resting on the raked glass and chromium windshield, was a small, slimly built man of about forty, wearing a white tropical suit that emphasized the rim of dark beard which framed his face. His black hair was brushed down over his bony forehead, and with his small eyes gave him a taut and watchful appearance. This man, Ventress—his name was about all Dr. Sanders had managed to learn about him—was the doctor's cabinmate. During the journey from Libreville he had roamed about the steamer like an impatient tiger, arguing with the steerage passengers and crew, his moods switching from a kind of ironic humor to sullen disinterest, when he would sit alone in the cabin, gazing out through the porthole at the small disc of empty sky.

Dr. Sanders had made one or two attempts to talk to him, but most of the time Ventress ignored him, keeping to himself whatever reasons he had for coming to Port Matarre. However, the doctor was well inured by now to being avoided by those around him. Shortly before they embarked, a slight contretemps, more embarrassing to his fellow passengers than to himself, had arisen over the choice of a cabinmate for Dr. Sanders. His fame having preceded him (what was fame to the world at large still remained notoriety on the personal level, Sanders reflected, and no doubt the reverse was true), no one could be found to share a cabin with the assistant director of the Fort Isabelle leper hospital.

At this point Ventress had stepped forward. Knocking on Dr. Sanders's door, suitcase in hand, he had nodded at the doctor and asked simply:

"Is it contagious?"

After a pause to examine this white-suited figure with his bearded skull-like face—something about him reminded Sanders that the world was not without those who, for their own reasons, wished to *catch* the disease —Dr. Sanders said: "The disease is contagious, as you ask, yes, but years of exposure and contact are necessary for its transmission. The period of incubation may be twenty or thirty years."

"Like death. Good." With a gleam of a smile, Ventress stepped into the cabin. He extended a bony hand, and clasped Sanders's firmly, his strong fingers feeling for the doctor's grip. "What our timorous fellow passengers fail to realize, Doctor, is that outside your colony there is merely another larger one."

Later, as he looked down at Ventress lounging in the speedboat on the afterdeck, Dr. Sanders pondered on this cryptic introduction. The faltering light still hung over the estuary, but Ventress's white suit seemed to focus all its intense hidden brilliancy, just as Father Balthus's clerical garb had reflected the darker tones. The steerage passengers milled around the speedboat, but Ventress appeared to be uninterested in them, or in the approaching jetty with its waiting throng of customs and police. Instead, he was looking out across the deserted starboard rail into the mouth of the river, and at the distant forest stretching away into the haze. His small eyes were half-closed, as if he were deliberately merging the view in front of him with some inner landscape within his mind.

Sanders had seen little of Ventress during the voyage up-coast, but one evening in the cabin, searching through the wrong suitcase in the dark, he had felt the butt of a heavy-caliber automatic pistol wrapped in the harness of a shoulder holster. The presence of this weapon had immediately resolved some of the enigmas that surrounded Ventress's small brittle figure.

"Doctor . . . " Ventress called up to him, waving one hand lightly, as if reminding Sanders that he was day-dreaming. "A drink, Sanders, before the bar closes?" Dr. Sanders began to refuse but Ventress had half-turned his shoulder, veering off on another tack. "Look for the sun, Doctor, it's there. You can't walk through these forests with your head between your heels."

"I shan't try to. Are you going ashore?"

"Of course. There's no hurry here, Doctor. This is a landscape without time."

Leaving him, Dr. Sanders made his way to the cabin. The three suitcases, Ventress's expensive one in polished crocodile skin, and his own scuffed workaday bags, were already packed and waiting beside the door. Sanders took off his jacket, and then bathed his hands in the washbasin, drying them lightly in the hope that the soap's pungent scent might make him seem less of a pariah to the examining officials.

However, Sanders realized only too well that by now, after fifteen years in Africa, ten of them at the Fort Isabelle hospital, any chance he may once have had of altering the outward aspect of himself, his image to the world at large, had long since gone. The work-stained cotton suit, slightly too small for his broad shoulders, the striped blue shirt and black tie, the strong head with its gray uncut hair and trace of beard—all these were the involuntary signatures of the physician to the lepers, as unmistakable as Sanders's own scarred but firm mouth and critical eye.

Opening the passport, Sanders compared the photograph taken eight years earlier with the reflection in the mirror. At a glance, the two men seemed barely recognizable—the first, with his straight, earnest face, his patent moral commitment to the lepers, all too obviously on top of his work at the hospital, looked more like the dedicated younger brother of the other, some remote and rather idiosyncratic country doctor.

Sanders looked down at his faded jacket and calloused hands, knowing how misleading this impression was, and how much better he understood, if not his present motives, at least those of his younger self, and the real reasons that had sent him to Fort Isabelle. Reminded by the birth date in the passport that he had now reached the age of forty, Sanders tried to visualize himself ten years ahead, but already the latent elements that had emerged in his face during the previous years seemed to have lost momentum. Ventress had referred to the Matarre forests as a landscape without time, and perhaps part of its appeal for Sanders was that here at last he might be free from the questions of motive and identity that were bound up with his sense of time and the past.

The steamer was now barely twenty feet from the jetty, and through the porthole Dr. Sanders could see the khaki-clad legs of the reception party. From his pocket he took out a well-thumbed envelope and drew from it a letter written in pale-blue ink that had almost penetrated the soft tissue. Both envelope and letter were franked with a censor's stamp, and panels which Sanders assumed contained the address had been cut out.

As the steamer bumped against the jetty, Dr. Sanders read through the letter for the last time on board.

Thursday, January 5th

My dear Edward,

At last we are here. The forest is the most beautiful in Africa, a house of jewels. I can barely find words to describe our wonder each morning as we look out across the slopes, still half-hidden by the mist but glistening like St. Sophia, each bough a jeweled semi-dome. Indeed, Max says I am becoming excessively Byzantine—I wear my hair to my waist even at the clinic, and affect a melancholy expression, although in fact for the first time in many years my heart sings! Both of us wish you were here. The clinic is small, with about twenty patients. Fortunately the people of these forest slopes move through life with a kind of dreamlike patience, and regard our work for them as more social than therapeutic. They walk through the dark forest with crowns of light on their heads.

Max sends his best wishes to you, as I do. We remember you often.

The light touches everything with diamonds and sapphires.

My love,
Suzanne

As the metal heels of the boarding party rang out across the deck over his head, Dr. Sanders read again the last line of the letter. But for the unofficial but firm assurances he had been given by the prefecture in Libreville, he would not have believed that Suzanne Clair and her husband had come to Port Matarre, so unlike the somber light of the river and jungle were her descriptions of the forest near the clinic. Their exact whereabouts no one had been able to tell him, or for that matter why a sudden censorship should have been imposed on mail leaving the province. When Sanders became too persistent, he was reminded that the correspondence of people under a criminal charge was liable to censorship, but as far as Suzanne and Max Clair were concerned, the suggestion was grotesque.

Thinking of the small, intelligent microbiologist and his wife, tall and dark-haired, with her high forehead and calm eyes, Dr. Sanders remembered their sudden departure from Fort Isabelle three months earlier. Sanders's affair with Suzanne had lasted for two years, kept going only by his inability to resolve it in any way. His failure to commit himself fully to her made it plain that she had become the focus of all his uncertainties at Fort Isabelle. For some time he had suspected that his reasons for serving at the leper hospital were not altogether humanitarian, and that he might be more attracted by the idea of leprosy, and whatever it unconsciously represented, than he imagined. Suzanne's somber beauty had become identified in his mind with this dark side of the psyche, and their affair was an attempt to come to terms with himself and his own ambiguous motives.

On second thought, Sanders recognized that a far more sinister explanation for their departure from the hospital was at hand. When Suzanne's letter arrived with its strange and ecstatic vision of the forest—in maculo-anesthetic leprosy there was an involvement of nervous tissue—he had decided to follow them. Forgoing his inquiries about the censored letter, in order not to warn Suzanne of his arrival, he took a month's leave from the hospital and set off for Port Matarre.

From Suzanne's description of the forest slopes he guessed the clinic to be somewhere near Mont Royal, possibly attached to one of the French-owned mining settlements, with their overzealous security men. However, the activity on the jetty outside—there were half a dozen soldiers moving about near a parked staff car—indicated that something more was afoot.

As he began to fold Suzanne's letter, smoothing the petal-like tissue, the cabin door opened sharply, jarring his elbow. With an apology Ventress stepped in, nodding to Sanders.

"I beg your pardon, Doctor. My bag." He added: "The customs people are here."

Annoyed to be caught reading the letter again by Ventress, Dr. Sanders stuffed envelope and letter into his pocket. For once Ventress appeared not to notice this. His hand rested on the handle of his suitcase, one ear cocked to listen to the sounds from the deck above. No doubt he was wondering what to do with the pistol. A thorough baggage search was the last thing any of them had expected.

Deciding to leave Ventress alone so that he could slip the weapon through the porthole, Dr. Sanders picked up his two suitcases.

"Well, goodbye, Doctor." Ventress was smiling, his face even more skull-like behind the beard. He held the door open. "It's been very interesting, a great pleasure to share a cabin with you."

Dr. Sanders nodded. "And perhaps something of a challenge too, M. Ventress? I hope all your victories come as easily."

"Touché, Doctor!" Ventress saluted him, then waved as Sanders made his way down the corridor. "But I gladly leave you with the last laugh—the old man with the scythe, eh?"

Without looking back, Dr. Sanders climbed the companionway to the saloon, aware of Ventress watching him from the door of the cabin. The other passengers were sitting in the chairs by the bar, Father Balthus among them, as a prolonged harangue took place between the first officer, two customs officials and a police sergeant. They were consulting the passenger list, scrutinizing everyone in turn as if searching for some missing passenger.

As Dr. Sanders lowered his two bags to the floor he caught the phrase: "No journalists allowed . . ." and then one of the customs men beckoned him over.

"Dr. Sanders?" he asked, putting a particular emphasis into the name as if he half hoped it might be an alias. "From Libreville University . . .?" He lowered his voice. "The Physics Department . . .? May I see your papers?"

Dr. Sanders pulled out his passport. A few feet to his left, Father Balthus was watching him with a sharp eye. "My name is Sanders, of the Fort Isabelle *léproserie*."

After apologizing for their mistake, the customs men glanced at each other and then cleared Dr. Sanders, chalking up his suitcases without bothering to open them. A few moments later he walked down the gangway. On the jetty the native soldiers lounged around the staff car. The rear seat remained vacant, presumably for the missing physicist from Libreville University.

As he handed his suitcases to a porter with *Hotel d'Europe* stenciled across his peaked cap, Dr. Sanders noticed that a far more thorough inspection was being made of the baggage of those leaving Port Matarre. A group of thirty to forty steerage passengers was herded together at the far end of the jetty, and the police and customs men were searching them one by one. Most of the natives carried bedrolls with them, and the police were unwinding these and squeezing the padding.

By contrast with this activity, the town was nearly deserted. The arcades on either side of the main street were empty, and the windows of the Hotel d'Europe hung listlessly in the dark air, the narrow shutters like coffin lids. Here, in the center of the town, the faded white façades made the somber light of the jungle seem even more pervasive. Looking back at the river as it turned like an immense snake into the forest, Dr. Sanders felt that it had sucked away all but a bare residue of life.

As he followed the porter up the steps into the hotel, he saw the black-robed figure of Father Balthus farther down the arcade. The priest was walking swiftly, his small traveling bag held in one hand. He turned between two columns, then crossed the road and disappeared among the shadows in the arcade facing the hotel. At intervals Sanders saw him again, his dark figure lit by the sunlight, the white columns of the arcade framing him like the shutter of a defective stroboscopic device. Then, for no apparent reason, he crossed the street again, the skirt of his black robe whipping the dust around his heels. His high face passed Sanders without turning, like the pale, half-remembered profile of someone glimpsed in a nightmare.

Sanders pointed after him. "Where's he off to?" he asked the porter: "The priest—he was on the steamer with me."

"To the seminary. The Jesuits are still there."

"Still? —what do you mean?"

Sanders moved toward the swinging doors, but at that moment a dark-haired young Frenchwoman stepped out. As her face was reflected in the moving panes, Sanders had a sudden glimpse of Suzanne Clair. Although the young woman was in her early twenties, at least ten years younger than Suzanne, she had the same wide hips and sauntering stride, the same observant gray eyes. As she passed Sanders, she murmured, "Pardon . . ." Then, returning his stare with a faint smile, she set off in the direction of an army lorry that was reversing down a side road. Sanders watched her go. Her trim white suit and metropolitan chic seemed out of place in the dingy light of Port Matarre.

"What's going on here?" Sanders said. "Have they found a new diamond field?"

The explanation seemed to make sense of the censorship and the customs search, but something about the porter's studied shrug made him doubt it. Besides, the references in Suzanne's letter to diamonds and sapphires would have been construed by the censor as an open invitation to join in the harvest.

The clerk at the reception desk was equally evasive. To Sanders's annoyance, the clerk insisted on showing him the weekly tariff, despite his assurances that he would be setting off for Mont Royal the following day.

"Doctor, you understand there is no boat, the service has been suspended. It will be cheaper for you if I charge you by the weekly tariff. But as you wish."

"All right." Dr. Sanders signed the register. As a precaution he gave as his address the university at Libreville. He had lectured several times at the medical school, and mail would be forwarded from there to Fort Isabelle. The deception might be useful at a later date.

"What about the railway?" he asked the clerk. "Or the bus service? There must be some transport to Mont Royal."

"There's no railway." The clerk snapped his fingers. "Diamonds, you know, Doctor, not difficult to transport. Perhaps you can make inquiries about the bus."

Dr. Sanders studied the man's thin, olive-skinned face. His liquid eyes roved around the doctor's suitcases and then out through the arcade to the forest canopy overtopping the roofs across the street. He seemed to be waiting for something to appear.

Dr. Sanders put away his pen. "Tell me, why is it so dark in Port Matarre? It's not overcast, and yet one can hardly see the sun."

The clerk shook his head. When he spoke, he seemed to be talking more to himself than to Sanders. "It's not dark, Doctor, it's the leaves. They're taking minerals from the ground, it makes everything look dark all the time."

This notion seemed to contain an element of truth. From the windows of his room overlooking the arcades, Dr. Sanders gazed out at the forest. The huge trees surrounded the port as if trying to crowd it back into the river. In the street the shadows were of the usual density, following at the heels of the few people who ventured out through the arcades, but the forest was without contrast of any kind. The leaves exposed to the sunlight were as dark as those below, almost as if the entire forest were draining all light from the sun in the same way that the river had emptied the town of its life and movement. The blackness of the canopy, the olive hues of the flat leaves, gave the forest a somber heaviness emphasized by the motes of light that flickered within its aerial galleries.

Preoccupied, Dr. Sanders almost failed to hear the knock on his door. He opened it to find Ventress standing in the corridor. His white-suited figure and sharp skull seemed to personify the bonelike colors of the deserted town.

"What is it?"

Ventress stepped forward. He held an envelope in his hand. "I found this in the cabin after you had gone, Doctor. I thought I should return it to you."

Dr. Sanders took the envelope, feeling in his pocket for Suzanne's letter. In his hurry he had evidently let it slip to the floor. He pushed the letter into the envelope, beckoning Ventress into the room. "Thank you, I didn't realize. . . ."

Ventress glanced around the room. Since disembarking from the steamer he had changed noticeably. The laconic and offhand manner had given way to a marked restlessness. His compact figure, held together as if all the muscles were opposing each other, contained an intense nervous energy that Sanders found almost uncomfortable. His eyes roved about, searching the shabby alcoves for some hidden perspective.

"May I take something in return, Doctor?" Before Sanders could answer, Ventress had stepped over to the larger of the two suitcases on the slatted stand beside the wardrobe. With a brief nod, he released the catches and raised the lid. From beneath the folded dressing gown, he withdrew his automatic pistol wrapped in its shoulder holster harness. Before Dr. Sanders could protest, he had slipped it away inside his jacket.

"What the devil—?" Dr. Sanders crossed the room. He pulled the lid of the suitcase into place. "You've got a bloody nerve . . .!"

Ventress gave him a weak smile, then started to walk past Sanders to the door. Annoyed, Sanders caught his arm and pulled the man almost off his feet. Ventress's face shut like a trap. With an agile swerve he feinted sideways on his small feet and wrenched himself away from Sanders.

As Sanders came forward again, Ventress seemed to debate whether to use his pistol and then raised a hand to pacify the doctor. "Sanders, I apologize, of course. But there was no other way. Try to understand me, it was those idiots on board I was taking advantage of—"

"Rubbish! You were taking advantage of *me!*"

Ventress shook his head vigorously. "You're wrong, Sanders. I assure you, I have no prejudice against your particular calling . . . far from it. Believe me, Doctor, I understand you, your whole—"

"All right!" Sanders pulled back the door. "Now get out!"

Ventress, however, stood his ground. He seemed to be trying to bring himself to say something, as if aware that he had exposed some private weakness of Sanders's and was doing his best to repair it. Then he gave a small shrug and left the room, bored by the doctor's irritation.

After he had gone Dr. Sanders sat down in the armchair with his back to the window. Ventress's ruse had annoyed him, not merely because of the assumption that the customs men would avoid contaminating themselves by touching his baggage. The smuggling of the pistol unknown to himself seemed to symbolize, in sexual terms as well, all his hidden motives for coming to Port Matarre in quest of Suzanne Clair. That Ventress, with his skeletal face and white suit, should have exposed his awareness of these still concealed motives was all the more irritating.

He ate an early lunch in the hotel restaurant. The

tables were almost deserted, and the only other guest was the dark-haired young Frenchwoman who sat by herself, writing into a dictation pad beside her salad. Now and then she glanced at Sanders, who was struck once again by her marked resemblance to Suzanne Clair. Perhaps because of her raven hair, or the unusual light in Port Matarre, her smooth face seemed paler in tone than Sanders remembered Suzanne's, as if the two women were cousins separated by some darker blood on Suzanne's side. As he looked at the girl he could almost see Suzanne beside her, reflected within some half-screened mirror in his mind.

When she left the table she nodded to Sanders, picked up her pad and went out into the street, pausing in the lobby on the way.

After lunch, Sanders began his search for some form of transport to take him to Mont Royal. As the desk clerk has stated, there was no railway to the mining town. A bus service ran twice daily, but for some reason had been discontinued. At the depot, near the barracks on the eastern outskirts of the town, Dr. Sanders found the booking office closed. The timetables peeled off the notice boards in the sunlight, and a few natives slept on the benches in the shade. After ten minutes a ticket collector wandered in with a broom, sucking on a piece of sugar cane. He shrugged when Dr. Sanders asked him when the service would be resumed.

"Perhaps tomorrow, or the next day, sir. Who can tell? The bridge is down."

"Where's this?"

"Where? Myanga, ten kilometers from Mont Royal. Steep ravine, the bridge just slid away. Risky there, sir."

Dr. Sanders pointed to the compound of the military barracks, where half a dozen trucks were being loaded with supplies. Bales of barbed wire were stacked on the ground to one side, next to some sections of metal fencing. "They seem busy enough. How are they going to get through?"

"They, sir, are repairing the bridge."

"With barbed wire?" Dr. Sanders shook his head, tired of this evasiveness. "What exactly is going on up there? At Mont Royal?"

The ticket collector sucked his sugar cane. "Going on?" he repeated dreamily. "Nothing's going on, sir."

Dr. Sanders strolled away, pausing by the barrack gates until the sentry gestured him on. Across the road the dark tiers of the forest canopy rose high into the air like an immense wave ready to fall across the empty town. Well over a hundred feet above his head, the great boughs hung like half-furled wings, the trunks leaning toward him. Dr. Sanders was tempted to cross the road and approach the forest, but there was something minatory and oppressive about its silence. He turned and made his way back to the hotel.

An hour later, after several fruitless inquiries, he called at the police prefecture near the harbor. The activity by the steamer had subsided, and most of the passengers were aboard. The speedboat was being swung out on a davit over the jetty.

Coming straight to the point, Dr. Sanders showed Suzanne's letter to the African charge captain. "Perhaps you could explain, Captain, why it was necessary to delete their address? These are close friends of mine and I wish to spend a fortnight's holiday with them. Now I find that there's no means of getting to Mont Royal, and an atmosphere of mystery surrounds the whole place."

The captain nodded, pondering over the letter on his desk. Occasionally he prodded the tissue with a steel ruler, as if he were examining the pressed petals of some rare and perhaps poisonous blossom. "I understand, Doctor. It's difficult for you."

"But why is the censorship in force at all?" Dr. Sanders pressed. "Is there some sort of political disturbance? Has a rebel group captured the mines? I'm naturally concerned for the well-being of Dr. and Madame Clair."

The captain shook his head. "I assure you, Doctor, there is no political trouble at Mont Royal—in fact, there is hardly anyone there at all. Most of the workers have left."

"Why? I've noticed that here. The town's empty."

The captain stood up and went over to the window. He pointed to the dark fringe of the jungle crowding over the rooftops of the native quarter beyond the warehouses. "The forest, Doctor, do you see? It frightens them, it's so black and heavy all the time." He went back to his desk and fiddled with the ruler. Sanders waited for him to make up his mind what to say. "In confidence, I can explain that there is a new kind of plant disease beginning in the forest near Mont Royal—"

"What do you mean?" Sanders cut in. "A virus disease, like tobacco mosaic?"

"Yes, that's it—" The captain nodded encouragingly, although he seemed to have little idea of what he was talking about. However, he kept a quiet eye on the rim of jungle in the window. "Anyway, it's not poisonous, but we have to take precautions. Some experts will look at the forest, send samples to Libreville—you understand, it takes time—" He handed back Suzanne's letter. "I will find out your friends' address. You come back in another day. All right?"

"Will I be able to go to Mont Royal?" Dr. Sanders asked. "The army hasn't closed off the area?"

"No—" the captain insisted. "You are quite free." He gestured with his hands, enclosing little parcels of air. "Just small areas, you see. It's not *dangerous*, your friends are all right. We don't want people rushing there, trying to make trouble."

At the door, Dr. Sanders asked: "How long has this been going on?" He pointed to the window. "The forest is very dark here."

The captain scratched his forehead. For a moment he looked tired and withdrawn. "About one year. Longer, perhaps. At first no one bothered . . ."

The jeweled orchid

On the steps outside, Dr. Sanders saw the young French-woman who had taken lunch at the hotel. She carried a businesslike handbag and wore a pair of dark glasses that failed to disguise the inquisitive look in her intelligent face. She watched Dr. Sanders as he walked past her.

"Any news?"

Sanders stopped. "What about?"

"The emergency."

"Is that what they call it? You're luckier than I. I haven't heard that term."

The young woman brushed this aside. She eyed Sanders up and down, as if unsure who he might be. "You can call it what you like," she said matter-of-factly. "If it isn't an emergency now, it soon will be." She came over to Sanders, lowering her voice. "Do you want to go to Mont Royal, Doctor?"

Sanders began to walk off, the young woman following him. "Are you a police spy?" he asked. "Or running an underground bus service? Or both, perhaps?"

"Neither. Listen." She stopped him when they had crossed the road to the first of the curio shops that ran down to the jetties between the warehouses. She took off her sunglasses and gave him a frank smile. "I'm sorry to pry—the clerk at the hotel told me who you were—but I'm stuck here myself and I thought you might know something. I've been in Port Matarre since the last boat."

"I can believe it." Dr. Sanders strolled on, eyeing the stands with their cheap ivory ornaments, small statuettes in an imitation Oceanic style the native carvers had somehow picked up at many removes from European magazines. "Port Matarre has more than a passing resemblance to purgatory."

"Tell me, are you on official business?" The young woman touched his arm. She had replaced her sunglasses, as if this gave her some sort of advantage in her interrogation. "You gave your address as the university at Libreville. In the hotel register."

"The medical school," Dr. Sanders said. "To put your curiosity at rest, if that's possible, I'm simply here on holiday. What about you?"

In a quieter voice, after a confirmatory glance at Sanders, she said: "I'm a journalist. I work free-lance for a bureau that sells material to the French illustrated weeklies."

"A journalist?" Dr. Sanders looked at her with more interest. During their brief conversation he had avoided looking at her, put off partly by her sunglasses, which seemed to emphasize the strange contrasts of light and dark in Port Matarre, and partly by her echoes of Suzanne Clair. "I didn't realize . . . I'm sorry I was offhand, but I've been getting nowhere today. Can you tell me about this emergency—I'll accept your term for it."

The young woman pointed to a bar at the next

corner. "We'll go there, it's quieter—I've been making a nuisance of myself all week with the police."

As they settled themselves in a booth by the window, she introduced herself as Louise Peret. Although prepared to accept Dr. Sanders as a fellow conspirator, she still wore her sunglasses, screening off some inner sanctum of herself. Her masked face and cool manner seemed to Sanders as typical in their way of Port Matarre as Ventress's strange garb, but already he sensed from the slight movement of her hands across the table toward him that she was searching for some point of contact.

"They're expecting a physicist from the university," she said. "A Dr. Tatlin, I think, though it's difficult to check from here. To begin with, I thought you might be Tatlin."

"A physicist—? That doesn't make sense. According to the police captain, these affected areas of the forest are suffering from a new virus disease. Have you been trying to get to Mont Royal all week?"

"Not exactly. I came here with another man from the bureau, an American called Anderson. When we left the boat he went off to Mont Royal in a hired car to take photographs. I was to wait here so I could get a story out quickly."

"Did he see anything?"

"Well, four days ago I spoke to him on the telephone, but the line was bad, I could hardly hear a thing. All he said was something about the forest being full of jewels, but it was meant as a joke, you know—" She gestured in the air.

"A figure of speech?"

"Exactly. If he had seen a new diamond field, he would have said so definitely. Anyway, the next day the telephone line was broken, and they're still trying to repair it—even the police can't get through."

Dr. Sanders ordered two brandies. Accepting a cigarette from Louise, he looked out through the window at the jetties along the river. The last of the cargo was being loaded aboard the steamer, and the passengers stood at the rail or sat passively on their luggage, looking down at the deck.

"It's difficult to know how seriously to take this," Sanders said. "Obviously something is going on, but it could be anything under the sun."

"Then what about the police and the army convoys? And the customs men out there this morning?"

Dr. Sanders shrugged. "Officialdom—if the telephone lines are down they probably know as little as we do. What I can't understand is why you and this American came here in the first place. By all accounts Mont Royal is even more dead than Port Matarre."

"Anderson had a tip that there was some kind of trouble near the mines—he wouldn't tell me what, it was really his story, you see—but we knew the army had sent in reserves. Tell me, Doctor, are you still going to Mont Royal? To your friends?"

"If I can. There must be some way. After all, it's only fifty miles, at a pinch one could walk it."

Louise laughed. "Not me." Just then a black-garbed figure strode past the window, heading off toward the market. "Father Balthus," Louise said. "His mission is near Mont Royal—I checked up on him too. There's a traveling companion for you."

"I doubt it." Dr. Sanders watched the priest walk briskly away from them, his thin face lifted as he crossed the road. His head and shoulders were held stiffly, but behind him his hands moved and twisted with a life of their own. "Father Balthus is not one to make a penitential progress—I think he has other problems on his mind." Dr. Sanders stood up, finishing his brandy. "However, it's a point. I think I'll have a word with the good Father. I'll see you back at the hotel—perhaps we can have dinner together?"

"Of course." She waved to him as he went out and then sat back against the window, her face motionless and without expression.

A hundred yards away, Dr. Sanders caught sight of the priest. Balthus had reached the outskirts of the native market and was moving among the first of the stalls, turning from left to right as if looking for someone. Dr. Sanders followed at a distance. The market was almost empty and he decided to keep the priest under observation for a few minutes before approaching him. Now and then, when Father Balthus glanced about, Sanders saw his lean face, the thin nose raised critically as he peered above the heads of the native women.

Dr. Sanders glanced down at the stalls, pausing to examine the carved statuettes and curios. The small local industry had made full use of the waste products of the mines at Mont Royal, and many of the teak and ivory carvings were decorated with fragments of calcite and fluorspar picked from the refuse heaps, ingeniously worked into the statuettes to form miniature crowns and necklaces. Many of the carvings were made from lumps of impure jade and amber, and the sculptors had abandoned all pretense to Christian imagery and produced squatting idols with pendulous abdomens and grimacing faces.

Still keeping Father Balthus under scrutiny, Dr. Sanders examined a large statuette of a native deity in which two crystals of calcium fluoride formed the eyes, the mineral phosphorescing in the sunlight. Nodding to the stall holder, he complimented her on the piece. Making the most of her opportunity, she gave him a wide smile and then drew back a strip of faded calico that covered the rear of the stall.

"My, that is a beauty!" Dr. Sanders reached forward to take the ornament she had exposed, but the woman held back his hands. Glittering below her in the sunlight was what appeared to be an immense crystalline orchid carved from some quartzlike mineral. The entire structure of the flower had been reproduced and then embedded within the crystal base, almost as if a living specimen had been conjured into the center of a huge cut-glass pendant. The internal faces of the quartz had been cut with remarkable skill, so that a dozen images of the orchid were refracted, one upon the other, as if seen through a maze of prisms. As Dr. Sanders moved his head, a continuous font of light poured from the jewel.

Dr. Sanders reached into his pocket for his wallet, and the woman smiled again and drew the cover back to expose several more of the ornaments. Next to the orchid was a spray of leaves attached to a twig, carved from a translucent jadelike stone. Each of the leaves had been reproduced with exquisite craftsmanship, the veins forming a pale lattice beneath the crystal. The spray of seven leaves, faithfully rendered down to the axillary buds and the faint warping of the twig, seemed characteristic more of some medieval Japanese jeweler's art than of the crude massive sculpture of Africa.

Next to the spray was an even more bizarre piece, a carved tree fungus that resembled a huge jeweled sponge. Both this and the spray of leaves shone with a dozen images of themselves refracted through the faces of the surrounding mount. Bending forward, Dr. Sanders placed himself between the ornaments and the sun, but the light within them sparkled as if coming from some interior source.

Before he could open his wallet there was a shout in the distance. A disturbance had broken out near one of the stalls. The stall holders ran about in all directions, and a woman's voice cried out. In the center of this scene stood Father Balthus, arms raised above his head as he held something in his hands, black robes lifted like the wings of a revenging bird.

"Wait for me!" Sanders called over his shoulder to the stall owner, but she had covered up her display, sliding the tray out of sight among the stacks of palm leaves and baskets of cocoa meal at the back of the stall.

Leaving her, Dr. Sanders ran through the crowd toward Father Balthus. The priest now stood alone, surrounded by a circle of onlookers, holding in his upraised hands a large native carving of a crucifix. Brandishing it like a sword over his head, he waved it from left to right as if semaphoring to some distant peak. Every few seconds he stopped and lowered the carving to inspect it, his thin face tense and perspiring.

The statuette, a cruder cousin of the jeweled orchid Dr. Sanders had seen, was carved from a pale-yellow gem-stone similar to chrysolite, the outstretched figure of the Christ embedded in a sheath of prismlike quartz. As the priest waved the statuette in the air, shaking it in a paroxysm of anger, the crystals seemed to deliquesce, the light pouring from them as from a burning taper.

"Balthus—!"

Dr. Sanders pushed through the crowd watching the priest. The faces were half averted, keeping an eye open for the police, as if the people were aware of their own complicity in whatever act of *lèse-majesté* Father Balthus was now punishing. The priest ignored them and continued to shake the carving, then lowered it from the air and felt the crystalline surface.

"Balthus, what on earth—?" Sanders began, but the priest shouldered him aside. Whirling the crucifix like a propeller, he watched its light flashing away, intent only on exorcising whatever powers it held for him.

There was a shout from one of the stall holders, and Dr. Sanders saw a native police sergeant approaching cautiously in the distance. Immediately the crowd began to scatter. Panting from his efforts, Father Balthus let one end of the crucifix fall to the ground. Still holding it like a blunted sword, he looked down at its dull surface. The crystalline sheath had vanished into the air.

"Obscene, obscene—!" he muttered to Dr. Sanders, as the latter took his arm and propelled him through the stalls. Sanders paused to toss the carving onto the blue sheet covering the owner's stall. The shaft, fashioned from some kind of polished wood, felt like a stick of ice. He pulled a five-franc note from his wallet and stuffed it into the stall owner's hands, then pushed Father Balthus in front of him. The priest was staring up at the sky and at the distant forest beyond the market. Deep within the great boughs the leaves flickered with the same hard light that had flared from the cross.

"Balthus, can't you see—?" Sanders took the priest's hand in a firm grip when they reached the wharf. The pale hand was as cold as the crucifix. "It was meant as a compliment. There was nothing obscene there—you've seen a thousand jeweled crosses."

The priest at last seemed to recognize him. His narrow face stared sharply at the doctor. He pulled his hand away. "You obviously don't understand, Doctor! That cross was not *jeweled!*"

Dr. Sanders watched him stride off, head and shoulders held stiffly with a fierce self-sufficient pride, the slim hands behind his back twisting and fretting like nervous serpents.

Later that day, as he and Louise Peret had dinner together in the deserted hotel, Dr. Sanders said: "I don't know what the good Father's motives are, but I'm certain his bishop wouldn't approve of them."

"You think he may have—changed sides?" Louise asked.

Laughing at this, Sanders replied: "That may be putting it too strongly, but I suspect that, professionally speaking, he was trying to confirm his doubts rather than allay them. That cross in the market drove him into a frenzy—he was literally trying to shake it to death."

"But why? I've seen those native carvings, they're beautiful but just ordinary pieces of jewelry."

"No, Louise. That's the point. As Balthus knew, they're not ordinary by any means. There's something about the light they give out—I didn't get a chance to examine one closely—but it seems to come from inside them, not from the sun. A hard, intense light, you can see it all over Port Matarre."

"I know." Louise's hand strayed to the sunglasses that lay beside her plate, safely within reach like some potent talisman. At intervals she automatically opened and closed them. "When you first arrive here everything seems dark, but then you look at the forest and see the stars burning in the leaves." She tapped the glasses. "That's why I wear these, Doctor."

"Is it?" Sanders picked up the glasses and held them in the air. One of the largest pairs he had seen, their frames were almost three inches deep. "Where did you get them? They're huge, Louise, they divide your face into two halves."

Louise shrugged. She lit a cigarette with a nervous flourish. "It's March 21, Doctor, the day of the equinox."

"The equinox? Yes, of course—when the sun crosses

the equator, and day and night are the same length—" Sanders pondered this. These divisions into dark and light seemed everywhere around them in Port Matarre, in the contrasts between Ventress's white suit and Balthus's dark soutane, in the white arcades with their shadowed in-fills, and even in his thoughts of Suzanne Clair, the somber twin of the young woman watching him across the table with her frank eyes.

"At least you can choose, Doctor, that's one thing. Nothing is blurred or gray now." She leaned forward. "Why did you come to Port Matarre? These friends, are you really looking for them?"

Sanders turned away from her level gaze. "It's too difficult to explain, I—" He debated whether to confide in her, and then with an effort pulled himself together. Sitting up, he touched her hand. "Look, tomorrow we must try to hire a car or a boat. If we share expenses it will give us longer in Mont Royal."

"I'll gladly come with you. But do you think it's safe?"

"For the time being. Whatever the police think, I'm sure it's not a virus growth." He felt the emerald in the gilt ring on Louise's finger, and added: "In a small way I'm something of an expert in these matters."

Without moving her hand from his touch, Louise said quietly: "I'm sure you are, Doctor. I spoke briefly this afternoon to the steward on the steamer." She added: "My aunt's cook is now a patient at your *léproserie*."

Sanders hesitated. "Louise, it's not *my léproserie*. Don't think I'm committed to it. As you say, perhaps we have a firm choice now."

They had finished their coffee. Sanders stood up and took Louise's arm. Perhaps because of her resemblance to Suzanne, he seemed to understand her movements as her hips and shoulders touching his own, as if familiar intimacies were already beginning to repeat themselves. Louise avoided his eyes, but her body remained close to him as they moved between the tables.

They walked out into the empty lobby. The desk clerk sat asleep with his head leaning against the small switchboard. To their left the brass rails of the staircase shone in the damp light, the limp fronds of the potted palms trailing onto the worn marble steps. Still holding Louise's arm, and feeling her fingers take his hand, Sanders glanced out through the entrance. In the shadows of the arcade he caught a glimpse of the shoes and trousers of a man leaning against a column.

"It's too late to go out," Louise said.

Sanders looked down at her, aware that for once all the inertia of sexual conventions, and his own reluctance to involve himself intimately with others, had slipped away. In addition he felt that the past day at Port Matarre, the ambivalent atmosphere of the deserted town, in some way placed them at a pivotal point below the dark and white shadows of the equinox. At these moments of balance any act was possible.

As they reached his door Louise drew her hand away and stepped forward into the darkened room. Sanders followed her and closed the door. Louise turned toward him, the pale light from the neon sign below illuminating one side of her face and mouth. Knocking her glasses to the floor as their hands brushed, Sanders held her in his arms, freeing himself for the moment from Suzanne Clair and the dark image of her face that floated like a dim lantern before his eyes.

Shortly after midnight, as Sanders lay asleep across the pillow on his bed, he woke to feel Louise touch his shoulder.

"Louise—?" He reached up and put his arm around her waist, but she disengaged his hand. "What is it—?"

"The window. Go to the window and look up to the southeast."

"What—?" Sanders gazed at her serious face, beckoning him across the room in the moonlight. "Of course, Louise—"

She waited by the bed as he crossed the faded carpet and unlatched the mosquito doors. Peering upward, he stared into the star-filled sky. In front of him, at an elevation of forty-five degrees, he picked out the constellations Taurus and Orion. Passing them was a star of immense magnitude, a huge corona of light borne in front of it and eclipsing the smaller stars in its path. At first Sanders failed to recognize this as the Echo satellite. Its luminosity had increased by at least tenfold, transforming the thin pinpoint of light that had burrowed across the night sky for so many faithful years into a brilliant luminary outshone only by the moon. All over Africa, from the Liberian coast to the shores of the Red Sea, it would now be visible, a vast aerial lantern fired by the same light he had seen in the jeweled flowers that afternoon.

Thinking lamely that perhaps the balloon might be breaking up, forming a cloud of aluminum like a gigantic mirror, Dr. Sanders watched the satellite setting in the southeast. As it faded, the dark canopy of the jungle flickered with a million points of light. Beside him Louise's white body glittered in a sheath of diamonds, the black surface of the river below spangled like the back of a sleeping snake.

Mulatto
on the
catwalks

In the darkness the worn columns of the arcade receded toward the eastern fringes of the town like pale ghosts, overtopped by the silent canopy of the forest. Sanders stopped outside the entrance of the hotel, and let the night air play on his creased suit. The faint odor of Louise's scent still clung to his face and hands. He stepped out into the road and looked up at his window. Unsettled by the image of the satellite, which had crossed the night sky like a warning beacon, Sanders had left the narrow, high-ceilinged hotel room and decided to go out for a walk. As he set off along the arcade toward the river, now and then passing the huddled form of a native asleep inside a roll of corrugated paper, he thought of Louise, with her quick smile and nervous hands, and her obsessional sunglasses. For the first time he felt convinced of the complete reality of Port Matarre. Already his memories of the *léproserie* and Suzanne Clair had faded. In some ways his journey to Mont Royal had lost its point. If anything, it would have made more sense to take Louise back to Fort Isabelle and try to work out his life afresh there in terms of her rather than Suzanne.

Yet the need to find Suzanne Clair, whose distant

presence, like a baleful planet, hung over the jungle toward Mont Royal, still remained. For Louise, too, he sensed that there were other preoccupations. She had told him something of her unsettled background, a childhood in one of the French communities in the Congo, and later of some kind of humiliation during the revolt against the central government after independence, when she and several other journalists had been caught in the rebel province of Katanga by mutinous *gendarmerie*. For Louise, as well as for himself, Port Matarre with its empty light was a neutral point, a dead zone on the African equator to which they had both been drawn. However, nothing achieved there, between themselves or anyone else, would necessarily have any lasting value.

At the end of the street, opposite the lights of the half-empty police prefecture, Sanders turned right along the river and walked toward the native market. The steamer had sailed for Libreville, and the main wharves were deserted, the gray hulls of four landing craft tied together in pairs. Below the market was the native harbor, a maze of small piers and catwalks. This water-borne shanty town of some two hundred boats and rafts was occupied at night by the stall holders in the market. A few fires burned from the tin stoves in the steering wells, lighting up the sleeping cubicles beneath the curved rattan roofs. One or two men sat on the catwalks above the boats, and a small group were playing dice at the end of the first pier, but otherwise the floating cantonment was silent, its cargo of jewelry eclipsed by the night.

The bar which Louise and he had visited the previous afternoon was still open. In the alleyway opposite the

entrance two African youths in blue denims were lounging around an abandoned motorcar, one of them sitting
on the hood against the windscreen. As Sanders entered
the bar they watched him with studied casualness.

The bar was almost empty. At the far end a European
plantation manager and his African foreman were talking to two of the local half-caste traders. Sanders carried
his whisky to a booth by the window, and looked out
across the river, calculating when the satellite would
make a second traverse.

He was thinking again of the jeweled leaves he had
seen in the market that afternoon, when someone
touched his shoulder and murmured: "Dr. Sanders?
You're up late, Doctor?"

Sanders turned to find the small, white-suited figure of
Ventress gazing down at him with his familiar ironic
smile. Remembering their brush the previous day,
Sanders said: "No, Ventress, *early*. I'm a day ahead of
you."

Ventress nodded eagerly, as if glad to see Sanders
gaining an advantage over him, even if only a verbal one.
Although he was standing, he seemed to Sanders to have
shrunk in size, his jacket tightly buttoned across his
narrow chest.

"That's good, Sanders, very good." Ventress glanced
around the deserted booths. "Can I join you for a
moment?"

"Well—" Sanders made no effort to be agreeable. The
incident with the automatic pistol reminded him of the
element of calculation in everything Ventress did. After
the past few hours with Louise the last person he wanted

near him was Ventress with his manic rhythms. "Could you—?"

"My dear Sanders, don't let me embarrass you! I'll stand." Oblivious of Sanders's half-turned shoulder, Ventress carried on. "How sensible of you, Doctor. The nights in Port Matarre are far more interesting than the days. Don't you agree?"

Sanders looked around at this, uncertain of Ventress's point. The man watching from the opposite arcade as he and Louise made their way up the staircase might well have been Ventress. "In a sense—"

"Astronomy isn't one of your hobbies, by any chance?" Ventress asked. He leaned over the table with his mock smile.

"I saw the satellite, if that's what you're driving at," Sanders said. "Tell me, how do you account for it—the sudden increase in magnitude?"

Ventress nodded sagely. "A large question, Doctor. To answer it I would need—literally, I fear—all the time in the world—"

Before Sanders could question him the door opened and one of the African youths he had seen by the car outside entered. A quick glance passed between himself and Ventress, and the youth slipped out again.

With a short bow at Sanders, Ventress turned and pulled his crocodile-skin suitcase from the booth behind Sanders. He paused on his way out and whispered at Sanders: "All the time in the world . . . remember that, Doctor!"

Wondering what it was that Ventress felt the need to hide behind these riddles, Dr. Sanders finished his whisky. Ventress's white figure, suitcase in hand, disappeared into the darkness near the piers, the two Africans moving quickly ahead of him.

Sanders gave him five minutes to make his departure, assuming that Ventress was about to leave by boat, whether hired or stolen, for Mont Royal. Although he would soon be following Ventress there, Sanders was glad to be left alone in Port Matarre. Ventress's presence in some way added an unnecessary random element to the already confused patterns of arcade and shadow, like a chess-game in which both players suspected that there was a concealed piece on the board.

As he walked past the abandoned motor-car, Sanders noticed that some sort of commotion was going on in the center of the native harbor. Many of the fires had been doused. Others were being fanned to life, and the flames danced in the disturbed water as the boats shifted and moved about. The overhead catwalks that crisscrossed the piers swayed under the weight of running men, swinging themselves along the handrails as they swerved after each other like shuttles.

Sanders moved closer to the edge of the water. Then he saw Ventress's small white figure darting about in the center of the chase, like a spider trapped in a collapsing web. Ventress shouted to the youth carrying his suitcase along the catwalk ten yards in front of him. A tall crop-haired mulatto in a khaki bush-shirt was swarming towards them, a length of weighted hose-pipe in his scarred hand. Behind Ventress the second youth had been beaten to the floor of the catwalk by two men in dark sweatshirts. Knives flashed in their hands, and the youth kicked at them and leapt sideways through the catwalk like a wriggling fish about to be gutted. He landed on a boat below, a long gash torn down the side of his denims. Holding the blood against his leg with one hand, he scrambled across the next boat to the pier, then ran off among the bales of cocoa meal.

On the catwalk above, Ventress shouted again, and the youth carrying the suitcase lifted the bag and feinted with it as the mulatto swung the hose-pipe at his head. Tossing the suitcase through the air in front of him, the youth slid below the rail and vaulted down on to the second rank of boats moored against the pier, crushing the rattan roof as he landed. The hovel collapsed in a mêlée of blankets and upturned petrol cans. There was a vivid glimmer as a cache of crystalline jewelry was exposed to the fires in the other boats.

Watching the brilliant jewels reflected in the broken water of the harbor as the lines of boats slipped from their moorings, Sanders heard the hard detonation of a gunshot sound out above the noise. The automatic pistol in his hand, Ventress crouched down on the catwalk. He fired again at the mulatto with the truncheon. As the mulatto backed away up a gangway to the wharf Ventress glanced over his shoulder at the two men behind him, both now motionless against the handrail, their dark bodies almost invisible. Holstering the pistol, Ventress lowered himself off the edge of the catwalk and leapt down on to the deck of the boat below.

Ignoring the boat's owner, a small gray-haired African trying to gather together the harvest of jeweled leaves scattered around him in the well of the boat, Ventress upended the trestle roof covered by a blanket. His two assistants had vanished among the boats between the next two piers, but Ventress seemed intent only on finding the suitcase. One by one he moved along the boats, kicking back the calico awnings, his pistol holding off the owners. As he stepped from one boat to the next a jeweled wake lay behind him. The three men on the catwalk above were reflected in the flaring light.

Giving up the hunt for his suitcase, Ventress pushed through the stall holders. He climbed up on to the pier. At its far end a small motor-boat lay moored by a single line to a sawn-off pile. Ventress reached the end of the pier, cast off the line and climbed into the boat. For a moment he worked at the controls, and the starting motor whined above the noise. A second later there was a jolting explosion from the bow locker of the boat, and a vivid geyser of flame lifted into the dark air. Knocked back against the tiller, Ventress looked up at the flames burning across the deck panels in front of the shattered windscreen. As the boat drifted back across the pier he managed to pull himself together and jumped up on to the floating box frame that served as a gangway.

Pushing past the few Africans watching from the shore, Sanders climbed on to the pier and ran towards Ventress. Hurt by the explosion, the white-suited man had not seen the pale outline of a large motor-cruiser that had been waiting out on the river some twenty yards from the end of the pier. Standing at the helm on the bridge, from where he had watched the pursuit across the catwalks, was a tall broad-shouldered man in a dark suit, his long face partly hidden behind the white shaft of the radio mast. On the deck below him was what appeared to be a yacht-club starting cannon, its squat polished barrel gleaming in the light. As the burning motor-boat drifted past the end of the pier the flames subsided, and the cruiser and its watching owner sank once again into the darkness.

Halfway along the pier Sanders saw the crop-headed mulatto swing down from the catwalk in front of him. He had thrown away the truncheon, and a thin silver blade flickered in his huge hand. He crept up behind Ventress, who sat numbly on the edge of the pier, watching the burning motor-boat move into the shallows.

"Ventress!" Running hard, Sanders caught up with the mulatto, and in his rush knocked the man off balance. Recovering with the speed of a snake, the mulatto lunged round and drove his shaved head at Sanders, hitting him in the chest. He bent down to retrieve his knife, his white eyes swinging from Ventress to the doctor and back again.

A hundred yards along the shore a signal flare rose into the air over the harbor. Its muffled light burned with a dull glow. A siren began to wail, its noise mounting over the warehouses. A police truck stopped at the foot of the next pier, and its headlights illuminated the last of the crystalline jewels now being hidden away beneath the awnings. The burning motor-boat had drifted against one of the catwalk supports, and the tar-streaked wood had caught fire, the flames flaring along the dry timbers.

Sanders lunged with one foot at the mulatto, then

wrenched at a half-loose timber sticking from the pier. The mulatto peered at the police truck. He seized the knife, then ran straight past Sanders along the pier and dived down among the boats on the far side.

"Ventress—?" Sanders knelt beside him, and brushed at the cinders that had burned themselves into the fabric of the man's suit. "Can you walk? The police are here."

Ventress stood up, his eyes clearing. Behind the beard, his small face seemed completely closed. He appeared to have no idea what had happened, and held on to Sanders's arm like an old man.

Behind them, out on the river, there was a muted roar, and white water broke behind the stern of the waiting cruiser. As it moved away Ventress came to life. Still holding Sanders's arm, but this time guiding him, he began to run along the pier.

"Head down, Doctor! We can't wait here!"

His head swivelled from left to right as he watched the burning catwalk, now dividing itself as it collapsed into the water. When they reached the bank and moved behind the small crowd standing on the slope he turned to Sanders: "My thanks, Doctor. I was almost out of time myself there."

Before Sanders could reply, Ventress darted off among the stacks of gasoline drums in the entrance to one of the warehouses. Sanders followed him, and saw Ventress disappear behind the abandoned motor-car.

In the harbor the fires had burned themselves out. The charred sections of the catwalk steamed and spat in the dark air. The police moved along the other catwalks with their machetes, cutting them one by one into the water, the stall holders below shouting as they paddled their boats out of the way.

Sanders walked back to his hotel, avoiding the arcades. Disturbed from their sleep, the mendicants sat up in their cardboard wrappings and wheedled at him as he went past, their eyes shining from the dark columns.

Louise had returned to her room. Switching off the light, Sanders sat down in the chair by the window. The last traces of Louise's scent dissolved in the air as he watched the dawn lift over the distant hills of Mont Royal, illuminating the serpentine course of the river as if revealing a secret pathway.

A
drowned
man

The next morning the body of a drowned man was taken from the river at Port Matarre. Shortly after ten o'clock Dr. Sanders and Louise Peret walked down to the harbor by the native market in the hope of hiring one of the boatmen to take them up-river to Mont Royal. The harbor was almost empty, and most of the boats had moved across the river to the settlements on the far bank. The wrecked catwalks lay in the water like the skeletons of half-drowned lizards, one or two of the fishermen poking around among them.

The market was quiet, either as a result of the incident the previous night or because Father Balthus's scene with the jeweled cross had dissuaded the owners of the curio stalls from putting in an appearance.

Despite the compacted glitter of the forest during the night, by day the jungle had become dark and somber again, as if the foliage were recharging itself from the sun. This pervading sense of unease convinced Sanders of the need to leave for Mont Royal with Louise as soon as possible. As they walked along he watched for any signs of the mulatto and his two assistants. However, from the scale of the attack upon Ventress—without doubt the armed motor-cruiser and its watching helms-

man had played some part in the attempted murder—
Sanders assumed that the would-be assassins were by
now a safe distance from the police.

During the short walk from the hotel Sanders had half-
expected to hear Ventress whisper to him from the
shadows within the arcade, but there had been no signs
of him in the town. However improbable, the unrelieved
heaviness of the light over Port Matarre convinced
Sanders that the white-suited figure had already left.

To Louise he pointed out the jumble of wrecked
catwalks and the charred hulk of the motor-boat lying in
the shallows, and described the attack by the mulatto
and his men.

"Perhaps he was trying to steal some jewelry from
the boats," Louise suggested. "They may just have been
defending themselves."

"No, it was more than that—this mulatto was really
after Ventress. If the police hadn't arrived we'd both
have ended up face down in the river."

"How horrible for you!" Louise took his arm, as if
barely convinced of Sanders's physical identity in the
nexus of uncertainty at Port Matarre. "But why should
anyone attack him?"

"I've no idea—you didn't find anything out about
Ventress?"

"No, I was following you most of the time. I haven't
even seen this small man with a beard. You make him
sound very sinister."

Sanders laughed at this. Holding her shoulders for a
few steps, he said: "My dear Louise, you have a Bluebeard complex—like all women. As a matter of fact,

Ventress isn't in the least sinister. On the contrary, he's rather naive and vulnerable—"

"Like Bluebeard, I suppose?"

"Well, not quite. But the way he talks in riddles all the time—it's as if he's frightened of revealing himself. I'd say he knew something about this crystallizing process."

"But why shouldn't he tell you directly? How could it have any bearing on his own situation?"

Sanders paused, glancing down at the sunglasses which Louise still carried in her hand. "Doesn't it with all of us, Louise? There are white shadows as well as black behind us in Port Matarre—why, God alone knows. Still, of one thing I'm sure, there's no actual physical danger from this process, or Ventress would have warned me. If anything, he was encouraging me to go to Mont Royal."

Louise shrugged. "Perhaps it would suit him to have you there."

"Perhaps—" They had passed the main piers of the native harbor, and Sanders stopped and spoke to the half-castes who owned the small group of fishing boats moored along the bank. They shook their heads when he mentioned Mont Royal, or seemed too unreliable to trust.

He rejoined Louise. "No good. They're the wrong kind of boats anyway."

"Is that the ferry over there?" Louise pointed a hundred yards along the bank, where half a dozen people stood at the water's edge near a landing stage. Two men armed with poles were steering in a large skiff.

When Louise and Dr. Sanders approached they saw that the boatmen were bringing in the floating body of a dead man.

The group of onlookers moved back as the body, prodded by the two poles, was beached in the shallows. After a pause, someone stepped forward and pulled it on to the damp mud. For a few moments everyone looked down at it, as the muddy water ran off the drenched clothing and drained from the blanched cheeks and eyes.

"Oooohh—!" With a shudder, Louise turned and backed away, stumbling a few feet up the bank to the landing stage. Leaving her, Dr. Sanders bent down to inspect the body. That of a muscular fair-skinned European of about thirty, it appeared to have suffered no external physical injuries. From the extent to which the dye had run from the leather belt and boots it was plain that the man had been immersed in water for four or five days, and Sanders was surprised to find that rigor mortis had still not occurred. The joints and tissues were malleable, the skin firm and almost warm.

What most attracted his attention, however, like that of the rest of the watching group, was the man's right arm. From the elbow to the finger tips it was enclosed by—or more precisely had effloresced into—a mass of translucent crystals, through which the prismatic outlines of the hand and fingers could be seen in a dozen multi-colored reflections. This huge jeweled gauntlet, like the coronation armor of a Spanish conquistador, was drying in the sun, its crystals beginning to emit a hard vivid light.

Dr. Sanders looked over his shoulder. Someone else had joined the watching group. Looking down at them from the top of the bank, his dark robe held below his hunched shoulders like the wings of a huge carrion bird, was the tall figure of Father Balthus. His eyes were fixed on the dead man's jeweled arm. A small tic in one corner of his mouth was fluttering, as if some blasphemous requiem for the dead man was discharging itself below the surface of the priest's consciousness. Then, with an effort, he turned on one heel and walked off along the river toward the town.

Dr. Sanders stood up as one of the watermen came forward. He stepped through the circle of onlookers and made his way to Louise Peret.

"Is that Anderson? The American? You recognized him."

Louise shook her head. "The cameraman, Matthieu. They went off in the car together." She looked up at Sanders, her face contorted. "His *arm?* What happened to it?"

Dr. Sanders moved her away from the group of people looking down at the body as the jeweled light discharged itself from the crystalline tissues. Fifty yards away, Father Balthus was striding past the native harbor, the fishermen stepping out of his path. Sanders gazed around, trying to take his bearings. "It's time to find out. Somewhere we've got to get hold of a boat."

Louise straightened her handbag, searching for her pencil and shorthand pad. "Edward, I think—I must get this story out. I'd like to go to Mont Royal with you, but with a dead man, it's not just guesswork any more."

"Louise!" Dr. Sanders held her arm. Already he sensed that the physical bond between them was slipping —Louise's eyes were turned away from him toward the body on the shore, as if she understood that there was little point in her going with Sanders to Mont Royal, and that his real motives for wanting to sail up-river, his quest for an end to all Suzanne Clair stood for in his mind, concerned him alone. Yet Sanders felt reluctant to let her go. However fragmentary their relationship, it offered at least an alternative to Suzanne.

"Louise, if we don't leave this morning we'll never get away from here. Once the police find that body they'll put a cordon around the whole of Mont Royal, if not Port Matarre as well." He hesitated, and then added: "That man had been in the water for at least four days, probably carried downstream all the way from Mont Royal, yet he died only half an hour ago."

"What do you mean?"

"Precisely that. He was still *warm*. Do you understand when I say we must leave for Mont Royal now? The story you want will be there, and you'll be the first—"

Sanders broke off, aware that their conversation was being overheard. They were walking along the quay, and to their right, twenty feet away, a motor-boat moved slowly through the water, keeping pace with them. Sanders recognized the red-and-yellow craft brought to Port Matarre on the steamer. Standing at the controls, one hand lightly on the steering helm, was a raffish-looking man with a droll handsome face. He eyed Dr. Sanders with a kind of amiable curiosity, as if balancing the advantages and drawbacks of becoming involved with him.

Dr. Sanders motioned to Louise to stop. The helmsman cut his engine, and the motor-boat drifted in an arc toward the bank. Dr. Sanders walked down to it, leaving Louise on the quay.

"A fine boat you have there," Sanders said to the helmsman.

The tall man made a deprecating gesture, then gave Sanders an easy smile. "I'm glad you appreciate it, Doctor." He pointed to Louise Peret. "I can see you have a good eye."

"Mlle. Peret is a colleague of mine. I'm more interested in boats just now. This one traveled with me on the steamer from Libreville."

"Then you know, Doctor, it's a fine craft, as you say. It could take you to Mont Royal in four or five hours."

"Excellent, indeed." Dr. Sanders glanced at his watch. "What would you charge for such a trip, Captain—?"

"Aragon." The tall man took a partly smoked cheroot from behind his ear and gestured with it at Louise. "For one? Or both of you?"

"Doctor—" Louise called down, still uncertain. "I'm not sure—"

"For the two of us," Dr. Sanders said, turning his back on the young woman. "We'll want to go today, within half an hour if possible. Now how much?"

For a few minutes they argued over the price, then agreed. Aragon started his motor, and shouted: "I'll see you at the next pier, Doctor, in an hour. The tide will have turned, it will carry us half the way."

At noon, their suitcases stowed away in the locker behind the engine, they set off up-river in the speed-boat. Dr. Sanders sat beside Aragon in the front seat, while Louise Peret, her dark hair flowing behind her in the slipstream, sat in one of the bucket seats behind. As they swept up the brown tidal river, the arcs of spray rainbowing behind them, Sanders felt the oppressive silence that had pervaded Port Matarre lift for the first time since his arrival. The deserted arcades, of which they had a last glimpse as they headed out into the main channel, and the somber forest seemed to recede into the background, separated from him by the roar and speed of the motor-boat. They passed the police wharf. A corporal lounging there with his squad watched them sweep by on a wake of foam. The powerful motor lifted the craft high out of the water, and Aragon leaned forward, watching the surface for any floating logs.

There were few other craft about. One or two native outriggers moved along by the edge of the banks, half hidden by the overhanging foliage. A mile from Port Matarre they passed the private jetties owned by the cocoa plantations. The empty lighters lay unattended under the idle cranes. Weeds sprang between the tracks of the small-gauge railways and climbed up the gantries of the storage silos. Everywhere the forest hung motion-less in the warm air, and the speed and spray of the motor-boat seemed to Dr. Sanders like an illusionist trick, the flickering shutter of a defective cine-camera.

Half an hour later, when they reached the tidal limits of the river, some ten miles inland, Aragon slowed down so that they could watch the water more closely. Dead trees and large pieces of bark drifted past. Now and then they came across sections of abandoned wharves that had been pulled off their moorings by the current. The river seemed untended and refuse-strewn, carrying the litter of deserted towns and villages.

"This is quite a boat, Captain," Dr. Sanders complimented Aragon, as the latter changed fuel tanks to preserve the balance of the craft.

Aragon nodded, steering the boat past the remains of a floating hut. "Faster than the police launches, Doctor."

"I'm sure it is. What do you use it for? Diamond-smuggling?"

Aragon turned his head, casting a sharp eye at Sanders. Despite the latter's reserved manner, Aragon seemed already to have made his own judgment of the doctor's character. He shrugged sadly. "So I hoped, Doctor, but too late now."

"Why do you say that?"

Aragon looked up at the dark forest draining all light from the air. "You'll see, Doctor. We'll soon be there."

"When were you last at Mont Royal, Captain?" Sanders asked. He glanced back at Louise. She leaned forward to catch Aragon's replies, holding her hair against her cheek.

"Not for five weeks. The police took my old boat."

"Do you know what's going on up there? Have they found a new mine?"

Aragon gave a laugh at this, and then steered the boat at a large white bird sitting on a log in their path. With a cry it took off straight over their heads, its huge wings working like ungainly oars. "You could say that, Doctor. But not in the way you mean." He added before

Sanders could question him further: "I really saw nothing. I was on the river, it was during the night."

"You saw the dead man in the harbor this morning?"

Aragon paused for half a minute before replying. At last he said: "El Dorado, the man of gold and jewels, in an armor of diamonds. There's an end many would wish for, Doctor."

"Perhaps. He was a friend of Mlle. Peret."

"Of Mlle.—?" With a grimace, Aragon sat forward over the helm.

Shortly after one thirty, when they were almost halfway to Mont Royal, they stopped by a derelict jetty that jutted out into the river from an abandoned plantation. Sitting on the soft beams over the water, they ate their lunch of ham and rolls followed by café royal. Nothing moved across the river or along the banks, and to Sanders it seemed that the entire area had been deserted.

Perhaps because of this, any conversation between them had lapsed. Aragon sat by himself, staring out at the water that swept past. The marked slope of his forehead, and his lean face with its pointed cheekbones, had given him a sharp piratical look along the waterfront at Port Matarre, but here, surrounded on all sides by the oppressive jungle, he seemed less sure of himself, more like some trigger-nerved forest guide. Why he had chosen to take Sanders and Louise to Mont Royal remained obscure, but Sanders guessed that he was drawn back to this focal area by motives as uncertain as his own.

Louise had also withdrawn into herself. As she smoked her cigarette after the meal she avoided Sanders's eyes. Deciding to leave her alone for the time being, Sanders walked away along the pier, picking his way across the broken boards until he reached the bank. The forest had re-entered the plantation, and the giant trees hung silently in lines, one dark cliff behind another.

In the distance he could see the ruined plantation house, creepers entwined through the rafters of the outbuildings. Ferns overgrew the garden of the house, running up to the doors and sprouting through the planks of the porch. Avoiding this mournful wreck, Sanders strolled around the perimeter of the garden, following the faded stones of a pathway. He passed the wire screen of a tennis court, the mesh covered by creepers and moss, and then reached the drained basin of an ornamental fountain.

Sanders sat down on the balustrade, and took out his cigarettes. He was looking across at the plantation house a few minutes later when he sat forward with a start. Watching him from an upstairs window of the house was a tall pale-skinned woman with a white mantilla covering her head and shoulders, the dark creepers clustering at the window around her.

Sanders threw away his cigarette and ran forward through the ferns. He reached the porch and kicked back the dusty frame of the door, then made his way toward the wide staircase. Here and there his shoes sank through the balsa-like boards, but the marble steps were still firm. The house had been stripped of its furniture and he crossed the landing upstairs to the bedroom in which he had seen the woman.

"Louise—!"

With a laugh she turned to face him, the puffy remains of an old lace curtain falling from one hand to the floor. Shaking her hair lightly, she smiled at Sanders.

"Did I frighten you?—I'm sorry."

"Louise—that was a damn silly thing to do—" With an effort Sanders controlled himself, his moment of recognition fading. "How the devil did you get up here?"

Louise sauntered around the room, looking at the patches left behind the pictures that had been removed, as if visiting some spectral gallery. "I walked, of course." She turned to face him, her eyes sharpening. "What's the matter—did I remind you of someone?"

Sanders went over to her. "Perhaps you did. Louise, it's difficult enough, without any practical jokes."

"It wasn't meant as a joke." She took his arm, her ironic smile gone. "Edward, I'm sorry, I shouldn't have—"

"Never mind." Sanders held her face to his shoulder, recovering himself in the physical contact with Louise. "For God's sake, Louise. All this will be over once we reach Mont Royal—before I had no choice."

"Of course—" She drew him away from the window. "Aragon—he can see us here."

The lace curtain lay on the floor at their feet, the mantilla Sanders had seen from the drained fountain in the garden. As Louise began to kneel down on it, holding his hands, he shook his head, then kicked it away into the corner.

Later, when they returned to the motor-boat, Aragon met them halfway down the pier. "We should leave, Doctor," he said, "the boat is exposed here—sometimes they patrol the river."

"Of course. How many soldiers are there in the Mont Royal area?" Sanders asked.

"Four or five hundred. Perhaps more."

"A battalion? That's a lot of men, Captain." He offered Aragon a cigarette from his case as Louise walked on ahead. "That incident in the native harbor last night—did you see it?"

"No, I heard this morning—those market boats are always catching fire."

"Perhaps. There was an attack on a man I know—a European called Ventress." He looked up at Aragon. "There was a large motor-cruiser with a cannon on the deck—you may have seen it on the river?"

Aragon's face gave nothing away. He shrugged vaguely. "It could belong to one of the mining companies. I haven't met this Ventress." Before Sanders could move on he added: "Remember, Doctor, there are many interests in Mont Royal that wish to stop people from going into the forest—or leaving it."

"I can see that. By the way, that drowned man in the harbor this morning—when you saw him, was he lying on a raft, by any chance?"

Aragon inhaled slowly on the cigarette, watching Sanders with some respect. "That's a good guess, Doctor."

"And as for this armor of light, was he covered with the crystals from head to foot?"

Aragon gave him a grimace of a smile, revealing a gold eye-tooth. He tapped it with his forefinger. " 'Covered' —is that the right word? My tooth is the whole gold, Doctor."

"I take the point." Sanders gazed down at the brown water sweeping past the polished timbers of the jetty. Louise waved to him from her place in the boat, but he was too preoccupied to reply. "You see, Captain, I'm wondering whether this man, Matthieu he was called, was dead in the absolute sense when you saw him. If, say, in the choppy open water of the harbor he had been knocked from the raft, but still held on in some way with one hand—that would explain a lot. It might have very important consequences. You see what I mean?"

Aragon smoked his cigarette, watching the crocodiles that lay in the shallows below the opposite bank. Then he threw the half-smoked cigarette into the water. "I think we should set off for Mont Royal now. The army here is not very intelligent."

"They have other things to think about, but you may well be right. Mlle. Peret thinks there is a physicist on the way. If so, he should be able to prevent any more tragic accidents."

Just before they started off Aragon turned to Dr. Sanders and said: "I was wondering, Doctor, why you were so eager to go to Mont Royal."

The remark seemed by way of apology for earlier suspicions, but Sanders found himself laughing defensively. With a shrug he said: "Two of my closest friends are in the affected zone, as well as Louise's American colleague. Naturally we're worried about them. The automatic temptation of the army will be to seal off the entire area and see what happens. They were loading barbed wire and fencing in the barracks at Port Matarre yesterday. For anyone trapped within the cordon it could be like being frozen solid inside a glacier."

The crystallized forest

Five miles from Mont Royal the river narrowed to little more than a hundred yards in width. Aragon reduced the speed of their craft to a few knots, steering between the islands of rubbish that drifted by, and avoiding the creepers that hung far out over the water from the high jungle walls on either side. Sitting forward, Dr. Sanders searched the forest, but the great trees were still dark and motionless.

They emerged into a more open stretch, where part of the undergrowth along the right-hand bank had been cut back to provide a small clearing. As Dr. Sanders pointed to a collection of derelict outbuildings, there was a tremendous blare of noise from the forest canopy above them, as if a huge engine had been mounted in the top-most branches, and a moment later a helicopter soared past above the trees.

It disappeared from view, its noise reverberating off the foliage. The few birds around them flickered away into the darkness of the forest, and the idling crocodiles submerged into the bark-stained water. As the helicopter hovered into view again a quarter of a mile ahead of them, Aragon cut the throttle and began to turn the craft toward the bank, but Sanders shook his head.

"We might as well carry on, Captain. We can't make it on foot through the forest. The farther we can go up-river the better."

As they continued down the center of the channel the helicopter continued to circle overhead, sometimes swinging up to a height of eight or nine hundred feet, as if to take a better look at the winding river, at other times soaring low over the water fifty yards in front of them, the wheels almost touching the surface. Then, abruptly, it zoomed away and carried out a wide circuit of the forest.

Rounding the next bend, where the river widened into a small harbor, they found that a pontoon barrage stretched across the channel from one bank to the next. On the right, along the wharves, were the warehouses bearing the names of the mining companies. Two landing craft and several military launches were tied up, and native soldiers moved about unloading equipment and drums of fuel. In the clearing beyond, a substantial military camp had been set up. The lines of tents ran off between the trees, partly hidden by the gray festoons of moss. Large piles of metal fencing lay about, and a squad of men were painting a number of black signs with luminous paint.

Halfway across the pontoon barrage a French sergeant with an electric megaphone called to them, pointing to the wharves. "A droite! A droite!" A group of soldiers waited by the jetty, leaning on their rifles.

Aragon hesitated, turning the boat in a slow spiral. "What now, Doctor?"

Sanders shrugged. "We'll have to go in. There's no point in trying to cut and run for it. If I'm going to find the Clairs, and Louise is to get her story, we'll have to do it on the army's terms."

They coasted in toward the wharf between the two landing craft, and Aragon threw the lines up to the waiting soldiers. As they climbed up on to the wooden deck the sergeant with the megaphone walked down the barrage.

"You made good time, Doctor. The helicopter only just caught up with you." He pointed between the warehouses to a small landing field by the camp. With a roar of noise, throwing up a tremendous fountain of dust, the helicopter was coming in to land.

"You knew we were coming? I thought the telephone line was down."

"Correct. But we have a radio, you know, Doctor." The sergeant smiled amiably. His relaxed good humor, uncharacteristic of the military in its dealings with civilians, suggested to Sanders that perhaps the events in the forest near by for once had made these soldiers only too glad to see their fellow men, whether in uniform or out.

The sergeant greeted Louise and Aragon, consulting a slip of paper. "Mlle. Peret? Monsieur Aragon? Would you come this way? Captain Radek would like a word with you, Doctor."

"Certainly. Tell me, Sergeant, if you have a radio how is it that the police at Port Matarre have no idea what's going on?"

"What *is* going on, Doctor? That's a question many people are trying to solve at this moment. As for the police at Port Matarre, we tell them as little as we think good for them. We're not eager to spread rumors, you know."

They set off toward a large metal hut that formed the battalion's headquarters. Dr. Sanders looked back at the river. Along the barrage across the channel two young soldiers walked to and fro with large butterfly nets in their hands, fishing methodically at the water that ran through the wire mesh hanging from the pontoons. More amphibious craft were moored against the wharf on the upstream side of the barrage, their crews sitting at the ready. The two landing craft sat low in the water, loaded almost to capacity with huge crates and bales, a random selection of household effects—refrigerators, air-conditioners and the like—and units of machinery and office cabinets.

As they reached the edge of the landing strip Dr. Sanders saw that the main runway consisted of a section of the Port Matarre–Mont Royal highway. Half a mile away the road had been sealed off by lines of fifty-gallon drums painted with black-and-white stripes. Beyond this point the forest sloped slowly upwards, giving way to the blue hills of the mining area. Lower down, by the river, the white roof-tops of the town shone in the sunlight above the jungle.

Two other aircraft, high-wing military monoplanes, were parked off the runway. The rotors of the helicopter had stopped and drooped downwards over the heads of a group of four or five civilians stepping unsteadily out of the cabin. As he reached the door of the hut Dr. Sanders recognized the black-garbed figure walking across the dusty ground.

"Edward!" Louise held his arm. "Who's that over there?"

"The priest. Balthus." Sanders turned to the sergeant as the latter opened the door. "What's he doing here?"

The sergeant paused for a moment, watching Sanders. "His parish is here, Doctor. Near the town. Surely we have to let him in?"

"Of course." Sanders collected himself. His sharp reaction to the arrival of the priest made him realize how far he already identified himself with the forest. He pointed to the civilians still finding their land-legs. "And the others?"

"Agriculture experts. They arrived at Port Matarre by flying boat this morning."

"Sounds like a big operation. Have you seen the forest, Sergeant?"

The sergeant held up his hand. "Captain Radek will explain, Doctor." He ushered Dr. Sanders across the corridor, then opened a door into a small waiting room and beckoned to Louise and Aragon. "Mlle.—please make yourself comfortable. I will have some coffee brought to you."

"But Sergeant, I have to—" Louise began to remonstrate with the sergeant, but Sanders put his hand on her shoulder.

"Louise, it's best if you wait here. I'll find out all I can."

Aragon waved to Sanders. "We'll see you later, Doctor. I'll keep an eye on your suitcases."

Captain Radek was waiting for Dr. Sanders in his office. A doctor in the army medical corps, he was plainly glad to find another physician in the neighborhood.

"Sit down, Doctor, it's a pleasure to see you. First of all, to put your mind at rest, may I say that an inspection party will be leaving for the area in half an hour, and I have arranged for us to go with them."

"Thank you, Captain. What of Mlle. Peret? She—"

"I'm sorry, Doctor, but that won't be possible." Radek placed his hands palm-downwards on the metal desk, as if trying to draw some kind of resolution from its hard surface. A tall slimly built man with somewhat weak eyes, he seemed anxious to come to a personal understanding with Sanders, the pressure of events making it necessary to dispense with the usual preliminaries of friendship. "I'm afraid we are keeping all journalists out of the area for the time being. It's not my decision but I'm sure you understand. Perhaps I should add that there are a number of matters I cannot confide to you— our operations in this area, evacuation plans and so forth—but I will be as frank as possible. Professor Tatlin flew here direct from Libreville this morning—he is at the inspection site now—and I'm sure he will be glad of your opinion."

"I'll be glad to give it," Dr. Sanders said. "It's not exactly my field of specialty."

Radek made a limp gesture with one hand, then let it fall back onto the desk. In a quiet voice, out of deference to any feelings Sanders might have, he said: "Who knows, Doctor? It seems to me that the business here and your own specialty are very similar. In a way, one is the dark side of the other. I'm thinking of the silver scales of leprosy that give the disease its name." He straightened up. "Now, tell me, have you seen any of the crystallized objects?"

"Some flowers and leaves." Sanders decided not to mention the dead man that morning. However frank and likeable the young army doctor might seem, Sanders's first priority was to reach the jungle. If they suspected him even of some remote complicity in Matthieu's death he might well find himself sidetracked into an endless military investigation. "The native market is full of them. They're selling them as curios."

Radek nodded. "This has been going on for some time—nearly a year, in fact. First it was costume jewelry, then small carvings and holy objects. Recently there's been quite a trade here—the natives were taking cheap carvings into the active zone, leaving them there overnight and going back the next day for them. Unfortunately some of the stuff, the jewelry in particular, had a tendency to dissolve."

"The rapid movement?" Dr. Sanders queried. "I noticed that. A curious effect, the discharge of light. Disconcerting to some of the wearers."

Radek smiled. "It didn't matter with the costume jewelry, but some of the native miners started using the same technique on the small diamonds they smuggled out. As you know, the diamond mines here don't produce gem-stones, and everyone was naturally surprised when these huge rocks began to reach the market. The share prices on the Paris Bourse climbed to fantastic heights. That's how it all started. A man was sent to investigate and ended up in the river."

"There were vested interests?"

"There still are. We aren't the only people trying to keep this quiet. The mines here have never been particularly profitable—" Radek seemed about to reveal something, and then changed his mind, perhaps aware of Sanders's withdrawn manner. "Well, I think I can tell you, in confidence of course, that this is not the only affected area in the world. At this moment at least two other sites exist—one in the Florida Everglades, and the other in the Pripet Marshes of the Soviet Union. Naturally, both are under intensive investigation."

"Then the effect is understood?" Dr. Sanders asked.

Radek shook his head. "Not at all. The Soviet team is under the leadership of Lysenko. As you can imagine, he is wasting the Russians' time. He believes that non-inherited mutations are responsible, and that because there is an apparent increase in tissue weight, crop yields can also be increased." Radek laughed wearily. "I'd like to see some of those tough Russians trying to chew a piece of this crystallized glass."

"What is Tatlin's theory?"

"In general he agrees with the American experts. I spoke to him at the site this morning." Radek opened a drawer and tossed something from it across the desk to Sanders. It lay there like crystallized leather, giving off a soft light. "That's a piece of bark I show to visitors."

Dr. Sanders pushed it back across the desk. "Thank you, but I saw the satellite last night."

Radek nodded to himself. He scooped the bark back into the drawer with his ruler and closed it, obviously glad to have this exhibit out of sight. He brushed his fingers together. "The satellite? Yes, an impressive sight. Venus now has two lamps. Not only two either. Apparently at the Mount Hubble Observatory in the States they have seen distant galaxies efflorescing!"

Radek paused, collecting his energies with an effort. "Tatlin believes that this Hubble Effect, as they call it, is closer to a cancer than anything else—and about as curable—an actual proliferation of the sub-atomic identity of all matter. It's as if a sequence of displaced but identical images of the same object were being produced by refraction through a prism, but with the element of time replacing the role of light."

There was a knock on the door. The sergeant put his head through. "The inspection party is ready to leave, sir."

"Good." Radek stood up and took his cap from the peg. "We'll have a look, Doctor. I think you'll be impressed."

Five minutes later the party of visitors, some dozen in number, set off in one of the amphibian craft. Father Balthus was not among them, and Sanders assumed that he had left for his mission by road. However, when he asked Radek why they were not approaching Mont Royal by the highway the captain told him that the road was closed. In response to Sanders's request, the captain arranged to make contact by field telephone with the clinic where Suzanne and Max Clair were working. The owner of the mine near by, a Swedish-American by the name of Thorensen, would tell them of Sanders's arrival, and with luck Max would be at the wharf to meet him when they landed.

Radek had heard nothing of Anderson's whereabouts. "However," he explained to Louise before they embarked, "we ourselves have had great difficulty in taking photographs—the crystals look like wet snow, in Paris they're still sceptical—so he may be hanging about somewhere, waiting for a convincing picture."

As he took his seat near the driver in the bow of the amphibian, Dr. Sanders waved to Louise Peret, who was watching from the wharf on the other side of the pontoon-barrage. He had promised to return with Max for her after they had visited the affected area, but even so Louise had made a half-hearted attempt to stop him going at all.

"Edward, wait till I can come with you—it's too dangerous for you—"

"My dear, I'm in good hands—the Captain will see everything is all right."

"There's no danger, Mlle. Peret," Radek assured her. "I will bring him back."

"I didn't mean—" She embraced Sanders hurriedly and walked back to where Aragon sat in the speedboat, talking to two of the soldiers. The presence of the barrage seemed to mark off one section of the forest from the other, a point beyond which they entered a world where the normal laws of the physical universe were suspended. The mood of the party was subdued, and the officials and French experts sat in a group at the stern, as if to place the maximum possible distance between themselves and whatever was to face them ahead.

For ten minutes they moved forward, the green walls of the forest slipping past on either side. They met a convoy of motor launches harnessed together behind a landing craft. All of them were crammed with cargo, their decks and cabin roofs loaded with household possessions of every kind, perambulators and mattresses, washing machines and bundles of linen, so that there were only a few inches of freeboard amidships. The solemn-faced French and Belgian children sat with suitcases on their knees above the freight. Their parents gazed expressionlessly at Sanders and his companions as they passed.

The last of the craft moved by, dragged through the disturbed water. Sanders turned and watched it go.

"You're evacuating the town?" he asked Radek.

"It was half-empty when we came. The affected zone moves about from one place to another, it's too dangerous for them to stay."

They were rounding a bend, as the river widened in its approach to Mont Royal, and the water ahead was touched by a roseate sheen, as if reflecting a distant sunset or the flames of a silent conflagration. The sky, however, remained a bland limpid blue, devoid of all clouds. They passed below a small bridge, where the river opened into a wide basin a quarter of a mile in diameter.

With a gasp of surprise they all craned forward, staring at the line of jungle facing the white-framed buildings of the town. The long arc of trees hanging over the water seemed to drip and glitter with myriads of prisms, the trunks and branches sheathed by bars of yellow and carmine light that bled away across the surface of the water, as if the whole scene were being reproduced by some over-active Technicolor process. The entire length of the opposite shore glittered with this blurred kaleidoscope, the overlapping bands of color increasing the density of the vegetation, so that it was impossible to see more than a few feet between the front line of trunks.

The sky was clear and motionless, the sunlight shining uninterruptedly upon this magnetic shore, but now and then a stir of wind crossed the water and the scene erupted into cascades of color that rippled away into the air around them. Then the coruscation subsided, and the images of the individual trees reappeared, each sheathed in its armor of light, foliage glowing as if loaded with deliquescing jewels.

Moved to astonishment, like everyone else in the craft, Dr. Sanders stared at this spectacle, his hands clasping the rail in front of him. The crystal light dappled his face and suit, transforming the pale fabric into a brilliant palimpsest of colors.

The craft moved in a wide arc toward the quay, where a group of launches were being loaded with equipment, and they came within some twenty yards of the trees, the hatchwork of colored light across their clothes transforming them for a moment into a boat-load of harlequins. There was a round of laughter at this, more in relief than amusement. Then several arms pointed to the water-line, and they could see that the process had not affected the vegetation alone.

Extending outwards for two or three yards from the

bank were the long splinters of what appeared to be crystallizing water, the angular facets emitting a blue and prismatic light washed by the wake from their craft. The splinters were growing in the water like crystals in a chemical solution, accreting more and more material to themselves, so that along the bank there was a congested mass of rhomboidal spears like the barbs of a reef, sharp enough to slit the hull of their craft.

A hubbub of speculation broke out in the launch, during which only Dr. Sanders and Radek remained silent. The captain was gazing up at the overhanging trees, encrusted by the translucent lattice, through which the sunlight was reflected in rainbows of primary colors. Unmistakably each tree was still alive, its leaves and boughs filled with sap. Dr. Sanders was thinking of Suzanne Clair's letter. She had written, "The forest is a house of jewels." For some reason he felt less concerned to find a so-called scientific explanation for the phenomenon he had just seen. The beauty of the spectacle had turned the keys of memory, and a thousand images of childhood, forgotten for nearly forty years, filled his mind, recalling the paradisal world when everything seemed illuminated by that prismatic light described so exactly by Wordsworth in his recollections of childhood. The magical shore in front of him seemed to glow like that brief spring.

"Dr. Sanders." Radek touched his arm. "We must go now."

"Of course." Sanders pulled himself together. The first passengers were disembarking from the gangway at the stern.

As he walked back between the seats Dr. Sanders started with surprise, pointing to a bearded man in a white suit who was crossing the gangway.

"There—! Ventress!"

"Doctor?" Radek caught up with him, peering solicitously into Sanders's eyes as if aware of the forest's impact. "Are you unwell?"

"Not at all. I . . . thought I recognized someone." He watched Ventress sidestep past the officials and make off down the quay, his bony skull held stiffly above his shoulders. A faint multi-colored dappling still touched his suit, as if the light from the forest had contaminated the fabric and set off the process anew. Without a backward glance, he stepped between two warehouses and disappeared among the sacks of cocoa meal.

Sanders stared after him, unsure whether he had in fact seen Ventress—had the white-suited figure been some kind of hallucination set off by the prismatic forest? It seemed impossible for Ventress to have smuggled himself aboard the craft, even by masquerading as one of the agriculture experts, though Sanders had been so distracted by the prospect of seeing the affected zone for the first time that he had not bothered to look closely at his fellow passengers.

"Do you wish to rest, Doctor?" Radek asked. "We can pause for a moment."

"If you like—" They stopped by one of the metal bollards. Sanders sat down on it, still thinking of the elusive figure of Ventress and its real significance. Again Sanders felt the sense of confusion which the strange light in Port Matarre had generated, a confusion in some way symbolized by Ventress and his skull-like face. Yet however much Ventress had seemed to reflect the flaring half-light in the town, Sanders was sure that here at Mont Royal the white-suited man would really come into his own.

"Captain—" Without thinking, Sanders said: "Radek, I wasn't entirely frank with you—"

"Doctor?" Radek's eyes were watching Sanders's. He nodded slowly, as if he already knew what Sanders would say.

"Don't misunderstand me." Sanders pointed to the forest glowing across the water. "I'm glad you're here, Radek. Before I was thinking only of myself. I had to leave Fort Isabelle—"

"I do understand you, Doctor." Radek touched his arm. "We must follow the party now." As they walked along the wharf, Radek said in his low voice: "Outside this forest everything seems polarized, does it not, divided into black and white? Wait until you reach the trees, Doctor—there, perhaps, these things will be reconciled for you."

The crash

Their party was divided into several smaller groups, each accompanied by two N.C.O.s. They moved off past the short queue of cars and trucks which the last of the European townsfolk were using to bring their possessions to the wharf. The families, those of the French and Belgian mine-technicians, waited their turn patiently, flagged on by the military police. The streets of Mont Royal were deserted, and the entire native population appeared to have long since vanished into the forest. The houses stood empty in the sunlight, shutters sealed across the windows, and soldiers paced up and down past the closed banks and stores. The side-streets were packed with abandoned cars, indicating that the river was the only route of escape from the town.

As they walked down to the control post, the jungle glowing two hundred yards away to their left, a large Chrysler with a dented fender swerved down the street and came to a halt in front of them. A tall man with blond hair, his double-breasted blue suit unbuttoned, climbed out. He recognized Radek and waved him over.

"This is Thorensen," Radek explained. "One of the mine-owners. It looks as if he hasn't been able to contact your friends. However, he may have news."

The tall man rested one hand on the roof of the car and scanned the surrounding roof-tops. The collar of his white shirt was open, and he scratched in a bored way at his neck. Although of powerful build, there was something weak and self-centered about his long fleshy face.

"Radek!" he shouted. "I haven't got all day! Is this Sanders?" He jerked his head at the doctor, then nodded to him. "Look, I got hold of them for you—they're at the mission hospital near the old Bourbon Hotel—he and his wife were supposed to come down here. Ten minutes ago he phoned that his wife's gone off somewhere, he has to look for her."

"Gone off somewhere?" Dr. Sanders repeated. "What does that mean?"

"How would I know?" Thorensen climbed into the car, forcing his huge body into the seat as if loading in a sack of meal. "Anyway, he said he'd be down here at six o'clock. O.K., Radek?"

"Thank you, Thorensen. We'll be here then."

With a nod, Thorensen jerked the car into reverse, backing it across the street in a cloud of dust. He set off at speed, almost running down a passing soldier.

"A rough diamond," Sanders commented. "If I can use the term here. Do you think he did get on to the Clairs?"

Radek shrugged. "Probably. Thorensen isn't exactly reliable, but he owed me a small favor for some medicines. A difficult man, always up to some game of his own. But he's been useful to us. The other mine-owners have gone but Thorensen still has his big boat."

Sanders looked around, remembering the attack on

Ventress in the harbor at Port Matarre. "A large motor-cruiser? With an ornamental cannon?"

"Ornamental? That doesn't sound like Thorensen." Radek laughed. "I can't remember his boat—why do you ask?"

"I thought I'd seen him before. What do we do now?"

"Nothing. The Bourbon Hotel is about three miles from here, it's an old ruin. If we go there we might not get back in time."

"It's strange—Suzanne Clair going off like that."

"Perhaps she had a patient to see. You think it was something to do with your coming here?"

"I hope not . . ." Sanders buttoned his jacket. "We might as well take a look at the forest until Max gets here."

Following the visiting party, they turned down the next side-street. They approached the forest, which stood back on either side of the road a quarter of a mile away. The vegetation was sparser, the grass growing in clumps along the sandy soil. In the open space a mobile laboratory had been set up in a trailer, and a platoon of soldiers was wandering about, taking cuttings from the trees, which they laid like fragments of stained glass on a line of trestle tables. The main body of the forest circled the eastern perimeter of the town, cutting off the highway to Port Matarre and the south.

Splitting up into twos and threes, they crossed the verge and began to walk among the glacé ferns which rose from the brittle ground. The sandy surface seemed curiously hard and annealed, small spurs of fused sand protruding from the newly formed crust.

A few yards from the trailer two technicians were spinning several of the encrusted branches in a centrifuge. There was a continuous glimmer as splinters of light glanced out of the bowl and vanished into the air. All over the inspection area, as far as the perimeter fence under the trees, the soldiers and visiting officials turned to watch. When the centrifuge stopped, the technicians peered into the bowl, where a handful of limp branches, their blanched leaves clinging damply to the metal bottom, lay stripped of their sheaths. Without comment, one of the technicians showed Dr. Sanders and Radek the empty liquor receptacle underneath.

Twenty yards from the forest, a helicopter prepared for take-off. Its heavy blades rotated like drooping scythes, sending up a blaze of light from the disturbed vegetation. With an abrupt lurch it made a labored take-off, swinging sideways through the air, and then moved across the forest roof, its churning blades gaining little purchase on the air. The soldiers and the visiting party stopped to watch the vivid discharge of light that radiated from the blades like St. Elmo's fire. Then, with a harsh roar like the bellow of a stricken animal, it slid backwards through the air and plunged tail-first toward the forest canopy a hundred feet below, the two pilots visible at their controls. Sirens sounded from the staff cars parked around the inspection area, and there was a concerted rush toward the forest as the aircraft disappeared from view.

As they raced along the road Dr. Sanders felt its

impact with the ground. A glow of light pulsed through the trees. The road led toward the point of the crash, a few houses looming at intervals at the ends of empty drives.

"The blades crystallized while it was near the trees!" Radek shouted as they climbed over the perimeter fence. "You could see the crystals deliquescing. Let's hope the pilots are all right!"

A sergeant blocked their way, beckoning back Sanders and the other civilians who were crowding along the fence. Radek shouted to the sergeant, who let Sanders go past, and then detached half a dozen of his men. The soldiers ran ahead of Radek and Dr. Sanders, stopping every twenty yards to peer through the trees.

They were soon within the body of the forest, and had entered an enchanted world. The crystal trees around them were hung with glass-like trellises of moss. The air was markedly cooler, as if everything was sheathed in ice, but a ceaseless play of light poured through the canopy overhead.

The process of crystallization was more advanced. The fences along the road were so heavily encrusted that they formed a continuous palisade, a white frost at least six inches thick on either side of the palings. The few houses between the trees glistened like wedding cakes, their white roofs and chimneys transformed into exotic minarets and baroque domes. On a lawn of green glass spurs a child's tricycle glittered like a Fabergé gem, the wheels starred into brilliant jasper crowns.

The soldiers were still ahead of Dr. Sanders, but Radek had fallen behind, limping along and pausing to feel the soles of his boots. By now it was obvious to Sanders why the highway to Port Matarre had been closed. The surface of the road was now a carpet of needles, spurs of glass and quartz five or six inches high that reflected the colored light from the leaves above. The spurs tore at Sanders's shoes, forcing him to move hand over hand along the verge.

"Sanders! Come back, Doctor!" The brittle echoes of Radek's voice, like a faint cry in an underground grotto, reached Sanders, but he stumbled on along the road, following the intricate patterns that revolved and expanded over his head like jeweled mandalas.

Behind him an engine roared, and the Chrysler he had seen with Thorensen plunged along the road, the heavy tires cutting through the crystal surface. Twenty yards ahead it rocked to a halt, its engine stalled, and Thorensen jumped out. With a shout he waved Sanders back down the road, now a tunnel of yellow and crimson light formed by the forest canopies overhead.

"Get back! There's another wave coming!" Glancing around wildly, as if searching for someone, he set off at a run after the soldiers.

Dr. Sanders rested by the Chrysler. A marked change had come over the forest, as if dusk had begun to fall. Everywhere the glacé sheaths which enveloped the trees and vegetation had become duller and more opaque. The crystal floor underfoot was occluded and gray, turning the needles into spurs of basalt. The brilliant panoply of colored light had gone, and a dim amber glow moved across the trees, shadowing the sequined floor. At the same time it had become considerably colder. Leaving the car, Dr. Sanders began to make his way back down the road—Radek was still shouting soundlessly to him— but the cold air blocked his path like a refrigerated wall. Turning up the collar of his tropical suit, Sanders retreated to the car, wondering whether to take refuge inside it. The cold deepened, numbing his face, and making his hands feel brittle and fleshless. Somewhere he heard Thorensen's hollow shout, and he caught a glimpse of a soldier running at full speed through the ice-gray trees.

On the right of the road the darkness enveloped the forest, masking the outlines of the trees, and then extended in a sudden sweep across the roadway. Dr. Sanders's eyes smarted with pain, and he brushed away the crystals of ice that had formed over the eyeballs. As his sight cleared he saw that everywhere around him a heavy frost was forming, accelerating the process of crystallization. The spurs in the roadway were over a foot in height, like the spines of a giant porcupine, and the lattices of moss between the trees were thicker and more translucent, so that the trunks seemed to shrink into a mottled thread. The interlocking leaves formed a continuous mosaic.

The windows of the car were covered by a heavy frost. Dr. Sanders reached for the door handle, but his fingers were stung by the intense cold.

"You there! Come on! This way!"

The voice echoed down a drive behind him. Looking around as the darkness deepened, Dr. Sanders saw the burly figure of Thorensen waving to him from the portico of a mansion near by. The lawn between them seemed to belong to a less somber zone, the grass still retaining its vivid liquid sparkle, as if this enclave were preserved intact like an island in the eye of a hurricane.

Dr. Sanders ran up the drive toward the house. Here the air was at least ten degrees warmer. Reaching the porch, he searched for Thorensen, but the mine-owner had run off again into the forest. Uncertain whether to follow him, Sanders watched the approaching wall of darkness slowly cross the lawn, the glittering foliage overhead sinking into its pall. At the bottom of the drive the Chrysler was now encrusted by a thick layer of frozen glass, its windshield blossoming into a thousand fleur-de-lis crystals.

Quickly making his way around the house, as the zone of safety moved off through the forest, Dr. Sanders crossed the remains of an old vegetable garden, where waist-high plants of green glass rose around him like exquisite sculptures. Waiting as the zone hesitated and veered off, he tried to remain within the center of its focus.

For the next hour he stumbled through the forest, his sense of direction lost, driven from left to right by the occluding walls. He had entered an endless subterranean cavern, where jeweled rocks loomed out of the spectral gloom like huge marine plants, the sprays of grass forming white fountains. Several times he crossed and re-crossed the road. The spurs were almost waist-high, and he was forced to clamber over the brittle stems.

Once, as he rested against the trunk of a bifurcated

oak, an immense multi-colored bird erupted from a bough over his head and flew off with a wild screech, aureoles of light cascading from its red and yellow wings.

At last the storm subsided, and a pale light filtered through the stained-glass canopy. Again the forest was a place of rainbows, a deep iridescent light glowing around him. He walked down a narrow roadway which wound toward a large colonial house standing like a baroque pavilion on a rise in the center of the forest. Transformed by the frost, it seemed an intact fragment of Versailles or Fontainebleau, its pilasters and friezes spilling from the wide roof like sculptured fountains.

The road narrowed, avoiding the slope which led up to the house, but its annealed crust, blunted like half-fused quartz, offered a more comfortable surface than the crystal teeth of the lawn. Fifty yards ahead Dr. Sanders came across what was unmistakably a jeweled rowing boat set solidly into the roadway, a chain of lapis lazuli mooring it to the verge. He realized that he was walking along a small tributary of the river, and that a thin stream of water still ran below the crust. This vestigial motion in some way prevented it from erupting into the spur-like forms of the rest of the forest floor.

As he paused by the boat, feeling the crystals along its sides, a huge four-legged creature half-embedded in the surface lurched forwards through the crust, the loosened pieces of lattice attached to its snout and shoulders shaking like a transparent cuirass. Its jaws mouthed the air silently as it struggled on its hooked legs, unable to clamber more than a few inches from the hollow trough in its own outline now filling with a thin trickle of water. Invested by the glittering light that poured from its body, the crocodile resembled a fabulous armorial beast. Its blind eyes had been transformed into immense crystalline rubies. It lunged toward him again, and Dr. Sanders kicked its snout, scattering the wet jewels that choked its mouth.

Leaving it to subside once more into a frozen posture, Dr. Sanders climbed the bank and limped across the lawn to the mansion, whose fairy towers loomed above the trees. Although out of breath and very nearly exhausted, he had a curious premonition of hope and longing, as if he were some fugitive Adam chancing upon a forgotten gateway to the forbidden paradise.

High in an upstairs window, the bearded man in the white suit watched him, the shotgun in his hands pointed at Sanders's chest.

II

The illuminated man

◆

Mirrors
and
assassins

Two months later, when describing the events of this period in a letter to Dr. Paul Derain, Director of the Fort Isabelle leper hospital, Sanders wrote:

—but what most surprised me, Paul, was the extent to which I was prepared for the transformation of the forest—the crystalline trees hanging like icons in those luminous caverns, the jeweled casements of the leaves overhead, fused into a lattice of prisms, through which the sun shone in a thousand rainbows, the birds and crocodiles frozen into grotesque postures like heraldic beasts carved from jade and quartz—what was really remarkable was the extent to which I accepted all these wonders as part of the natural order of things, part of the inward pattern of the universe. True, to begin with I was as startled as everyone else making his first journey up the Matarre River to Mont Royal, but after the initial impact of the forest, a surprise more visual than anything else, I quickly came to understand it, knowing that its hazards were a small price to pay for its illumination of my life. Indeed, the rest of the world seemed drab and inert by contrast, a faded reflection of this bright image, forming a gray penumbral zone like some half-abandoned purgatory.

All this, my dear Paul, the very absence of surprise, confirms my belief that this illuminated forest in some way reflects an earlier period of our lives, perhaps an archaic memory we are born with of some ancestral paradise where the unity of time and space is the signature of every leaf and flower. It's obvious to everyone now that in the forest life and death have a different meaning from that in our ordinary lack-lustre world. Here we have always associated movement with life and the passage of time, but from my experience within the forest near Mont Royal I know that all motion leads inevitably to death, and that time is its servant.

It is, perhaps, our unique achievement as lords of this creation to have brought about the separation of time and space. We alone have given to each a separate value, a distinct measure of their own which now define and bind us like the length and breadth of a coffin. To resolve them again is the greatest aim of natural science—as you and I have seen, Paul, in our work on the virus, with its semi-animate, crystalline existence, half-in and half-out of our own time-stream, as if intersecting it at an angle— often I think that in our microscopes, examining the tissues of those poor lepers in our hospital, we were looking upon a minuscule replica of the world I was to meet later in the forest slopes near Mont Royal.

However, all these belated efforts have now been brought to an end. As I write to you, here within the quiet and emptiness of the Hotel d'Europe at Port Matarre, I see a report in a two-week-old issue of *Paris-Soir* (Louise Peret, the young Frenchwoman who is with me here, doing her best to look after the wayward whims of your former assistant, had hidden the paper from me for a week) that the whole of the Florida peninsula in the United States, with the exception of a single highway to Tampa, has been closed, and that to date some three million of the state's inhabitants have been resettled in other parts of the country.

But apart from the estimated losses in real-estate values and hotel revenues ("Oh, Miami," I cannot help saying to myself, "you city of a thousand cathedrals to the rainbow sun!") the news of this extraordinary human migration has prompted little comment. Such is mankind's innate optimism, our conviction that we can survive any deluge or cataclysm, that most of us unconsciously dismiss the momentous events in Florida with a shrug, confident that some means will be found to avert the crisis when it comes.

And yet, Paul, it now seems obvious that the real crisis is long past. Tucked away on the back page of the same issue of *Paris-Soir* is the short report of the sighting of another "double galaxy" by observers of the Hubble Institute on Mount Palomar. The news is summarized in less than a dozen lines and without comment, although the implication is inescapable that yet another focal area has been set up somewhere on the surface of the earth, in the temple-filled jungles of Cambodia or the haunted amber forests of the Chilean highland. But it is still only a year since the Mount Palomar astronomers identified the first double galaxy in the constellation Andromeda, the great oblate diadem that is probably the most beautiful object in the physical universe, the island galaxy M 31. Without doubt, these random transfigurations throughout the world are a reflection of distant cosmic processes of enormous scope and dimensions, first glimpsed in the Andromeda spiral.

We now know that it is time ("time with the Midas touch," as Ventress described it) which is responsible for the transformation. The recent discovery of anti-matter in the universe inevitably involves the conception of anti-time as the fourth side of this negatively charged continuum. Where anti-particle and particle collide they not only destroy their own physical identities, but their opposing time-values eliminate each other, subtracting from the universe another quantum from its total store of time. It is random discharges of this type, set off by the creation of anti-galaxies in space, which have led to the depletion of the time-store available to the materials of our own solar system.

Just as a super-saturated solution will discharge itself into a crystalline mass, so the super-saturation of matter in our continuum leads to its appearance in a parallel spatial matrix. As more and more time "leaks" away, the process of super-saturation continues, the original atoms and molecules producing spatial replicas of themselves, substance without mass, in an attempt to increase their foot-hold upon existence. The process is theoretically without end, and it may be possible eventually for a single atom to produce an infinite number of duplicates of itself and so fill the entire universe, from which simultaneously all time has expired, an ultimate macrocosmic zero beyond the wildest dreams of Plato and Democritus.

In parenthesis: reading this over my shoulder, Louise comments that I may be misleading you, Paul, by minimizing the dangers we all experienced within the crystalline forest. It's certainly true that they were very real at the time, as the many tragic deaths there testify, and that first day when I was trapped in the forest I understood nothing of these matters, beyond those which Ventress confided to me in his ambiguous and disjointed way. But even then, as I walked away from that jeweled crocodile up the sloping lawn towards the white-suited man watching me from the window, his shotgun pointed at my chest—

Lying back on one of the glass-embroidered chester-fields in the bedroom upstairs, Dr. Sanders rested after his chase through the forest. As he climbed the staircase he had slipped on one of the crystallizing steps and momentarily winded himself. Standing at the top of the staircase, Ventress had watched him clamber to his feet, the glacé panels splintering under his hands. Ventress's small face, the tight skin now mottled by vein-like colors, was without expression. His eyes gazed down, showing not even a flicker of response as Sanders grappled for his balance at the banisters. When Sanders at last reached the landing Ventress motioned him toward the floor with a curt gesture. He then took up his position at the window, driving the butt of the shotgun through the broken panes as they annealed themselves.

Dr. Sanders brushed the frost off his suit, picking at the crystal splinters embedded like needles in his hands. The air in the house was cold and motionless, but as the storm subsided, moving away across the forest, the process of vitrification seemed to diminish. Everything in the high-ceilinged room had been transformed by the frost. Several plate-glass windows appeared to have been fractured and then fused together above the carpet, and the ornate Persian patterns swam below the surface like the floor of some perfumed pool in the *Arabian Nights*. All the furniture was covered by the same glacé sheath, the arms and legs of the straight-backed chairs against the walls embellished by exquisite curlicues and helixes. The imitation Louis XV pieces had been transformed into huge fragments of opalescent candy, whose multiple reflections glowed like giant chimeras in the cut-glass walls.

Through the doorway opposite, Dr. Sanders could see into a small dressing-room. He assumed he was sitting in the principal bedroom of an official residence maintained for some visiting government dignitary or the president of one of the mine companies. Although elaborately furnished—straight from the catalogues of a Paris or London department store—the room was devoid of all personal possessions. For some reason, the large double bed—a four-poster, Sanders guessed from the patch on the ceiling—had been removed, and the other furniture pushed to one side by Ventress. He still stood by the open window, peering down at the stream where the jeweled boat and the crocodile lay embalmed. His thin beard gave him a fevered and haunted aspect. Half-bent over his shotgun, he pressed closer to the window, ignoring the sections of crystal sheath that he dislodged from the heavy brocaded curtain.

Dr. Sanders began to stand up, but Ventress waved him back.

"Rest yourself, Doctor. We'll be here for some time." His voice had become harder and the gloss of ironic humor was absent. He glanced away from his gun-barrel. "When did you last see Thorensen?"

"The mine-owner?" Sanders pointed through the window. "After we ran to search for the helicopter. Are you looking for him?"

"In a manner of speaking. What was he doing?"

Dr. Sanders turned up the collar of his jacket, brushing away the fine spurs of frost that covered the material. "He was running around in circles like the rest of us, completely lost."

"Lost?" Ventress let out a derisive snort. "The man's as cunning as a pig! He knows every dell and cranny of this forest like the back of his hand."

When Sanders stood up and approached the window Ventress beckoned him away impatiently. "Keep away from the window, Doctor." With a brief gleam of his old ironic humor, he added: "I don't want to use you as a decoy just yet."

Ignoring this warning, Sanders glanced down at the empty lawn. Like footsteps in dew-covered grass, the dark prints of his shoes crossed the sequined surface, merging into the pale-green slope as the process of crystallization continued. Although the main wave of activity had moved off, the forest was still vitrifying itself. The absolute silence of the jeweled trees seemed to confirm that the affected area had multiplied many times in size. A frozen calm extended as far as he could see, as if he and Ventress were lost somewhere in the grottoes of an immense glacier. To emphasize their proximity to the sun, everywhere there was the same corona of light. The forest was an endless labyrinth of glass caves, sealed off from the remainder of the world and lit by subterranean lamps.

Ventress relaxed for a moment. Raising one foot to the window-sill, he surveyed Dr. Sanders. "A long journey, Doctor, but one worth making?"

Sanders shrugged. "I haven't reached the end of it yet, by any means—I've still got to find my friends. However, I agree with you, it's an extraordinary experience. There's something almost rejuvenating about the forest. Do you—?"

"Of course, Doctor." Ventress turned back to the window, silencing Sanders with one hand. The frost glimmered on the shoulders of his white suit in a faint palimpsest of colors. He peered down at the crystal vegetation along the stream. After a pause he said: "My dear Sanders, you're not the only one to feel these things, let me assure you."

"You've been here before?" Sanders asked.

"Do you mean—*déjà vu?*" Ventress looked round, his small features almost hidden behind the beard. Dr. Sanders hesitated. "I meant literally," he said.

Ventress ignored this. "We've all been here before, Doctor, as everyone will soon find out—if there's *time*." He pronounced the word with a peculiar inflexion of his own, drawing it out like the tolling of a bell. He listened to the last echoes reverberate away among the crystal walls, like a fading requiem. "However, I feel that's something we're all running out of, Doctor—do you agree?"

Dr. Sanders tried to massage some warmth into his hands. His fingers felt brittle and fleshless, and he looked at the empty fireplace behind him, wondering whether this ornate recess, guarded on either side by a large gilt dolphin, had been fitted with a chimney flue. Yet despite the cold air in the house he felt less chilled than invigorated.

"Running out of time?" he repeated. "I haven't thought about it yet. What's your explanation?"

"Isn't it obvious, Doctor? Doesn't your own 'specialty,' the dark side of the sun we see around us here, provide a clue? Surely leprosy, like cancer, is above all a disease of time, a result of over-extending oneself through that particular medium?"

Dr. Sanders nodded as Ventress spoke, watching the man's skull-like face come alive as he discussed this element that he appeared, on the surface at least, to despise. "It's a theory," he agreed when Ventress had finished. "Not—"

"Not scientific enough?" Ventress threw his head back. In a louder voice, he declaimed: "Look at the viruses, Doctor, with their crystalline structure, neither animate nor inanimate, and their immunity to time!" He swept a hand along the sill and scooped up a cluster of the vitreous grains, then scattered them across the floor like smashed marbles. "You and I will be like them soon, Sanders, and the rest of the world. Neither living nor dead!"

At the end of this tirade Ventress turned away and resumed his scrutiny of the forest. A muscle flickered in his left cheek, like distant lightning marking the end of a storm.

"Why are you looking for Thorensen?" Dr. Sanders asked. "Are you after his diamond mine?"

"Don't be a fool!" Ventress swore over his shoulder. "That's the last thing—gem-stones are no rarity in this forest, Doctor." With a comtemptuous gesture he scraped a mass of crystals from the material of his suit. "If you want I'll pluck you a necklace of Hope diamonds."

"What are you doing here?" Dr. Sanders asked evenly. "In this house?"

"Thorensen lives here."

"What?" Incredulously, Sanders looked again at the ornate furniture and gilded mirrors, thinking of the burly man in the blue suit at the wheel of the dented Chrysler. "I saw him for only a few moments, but it doesn't seem in character."

"Precisely. I've never seen such bad taste." Ventress nodded to himself. "And believe me, as an architect I've seen plenty. The whole house is a pathetic joke." He pointed to one of the marquetry divans with a spiral bolster that had transformed itself into a brilliant parody of a rococo cartouche, the helix twisting like the overgrown horns of a goat. "Louis Nineteen, perhaps?"

Carried away by his jibes at the absent Thorensen, Ventress had turned his back on the window. Looking past him, Dr. Sanders saw the crocodile trapped in the stream lift on its weak legs, as if snapping at a passer-by. Interrupting Ventress, Sanders pointed down at it, but another voice anticipated him.

"Ventress!"

The shout, an angry challenge, came from the crystal shrubbery along the left-hand margins of the lawn. A second later a shot roared out into the cold air. As Ventress swung round, pushing Sanders away with one hand, the bullet crashed into the ceiling over their heads, bringing down a huge lattice-like section that splintered around their feet into a mass of flattened needles. Ventress flinched back, and then blindly fired off a shot at the shrubbery. The report echoed around the petrified trees, shaking loose their vivid colors.

"Keep down!" Ventress scuttled along the floor to the next window, then worked the barrel of the shotgun through the frosted panes. After his initial moment of stunned panic he had recovered his wits, and even seemed to seize on this chance of a confrontation. He peered down at the garden, then stood up when the cracking of a distant tree appeared to mark the retreat of their hidden assailant.

Ventress walked across to Sanders, who was standing with his back to the wall beside the window.

"All right. He's gone."

Sanders hesitated before moving. He glanced around the trees at the edges of the lawn, trying not to expose more than a glimpse of himself. At the far end of the lawn, framed between two oaks, a white gazebo had been transformed by the frost into a huge crystal crown. Its glass casements winked like inlaid jewels, as if something were moving behind them. Ventress, however, stood openly in front of the window, surveying the scene below.

"Was that Thorensen?" Sanders asked.

"Of course." This brief passage-at-arms seemed to have relaxed Ventress. The shotgun cradled loosely in his elbow, he strolled around the room, now and then pausing to examine the puncture left by the bullet in the ceiling. For some reason he obviously assumed that Sanders had taken his side in this private duel, perhaps because Sanders had already saved him from the attack in the native harbor at Port Matarre. Sanders's actions, however, had been little more than reflex, as Ventress no doubt was aware. Patently Ventress was not a man who ever felt under much obligation to other people, whatever they might have done for him, and Sanders guessed that in fact Ventress had sensed some spark of kinship during their voyage by steamer from Libreville and that he would plunge his entire sympathy or hostility upon such a chance encounter.

The movement inside the gazebo had ended. Sanders stepped forward from his hiding place behind the window.

"The attack on you in Port Matarre—were those Thorensen's men?"

Ventress shrugged. "You might well be right, Doctor. Don't worry, I'll look after you."

"You'll have your work cut out—those thugs meant business. From what the army captain at the base told me the diamond companies don't intend to let anything get in their way."

Ventress shook his head, exasperated by Sanders's obtuseness. "Doctor! You persist in finding the most trivial reasons—obviously you have no idea of your real motives! For the last time, I am not interested in Thorensen's damned diamonds—and nor is Thorensen! The matter between us—" He broke off, staring vaguely through the window, his face for the first time showing any sign of fatigue. In a distracted voice, more to himself, he went on: "Believe me, I respect Thorensen—however crude, he understands that we have the same aim, it's a question of method—" Ventress swung on his heel. "We'd better leave now," he announced. "There's no point in staying. Where are you going?"

"Mont Royal, if that's possible."

"It won't be." Ventress pointed through the window.

"The storm center is directly between here and the town. Your only hope is to reach the river and follow it back to the army base. Whom are you looking for?"

"A former colleague of mine and his wife. Do you know the Bourbon Hotel? It's some distance from the town. Their mission hospital is near the hotel."

"Bourbon?" Ventress screwed up his face. "Sounds like the wrong century—you're out of time again, Sanders." He made for the door. "It's an old ruin, God only knows where. You'll have to stay with me until we reach the edge of the forest, then work your way back to the army base."

Testing each step, they went down the crystallizing staircase. Halfway down, Ventress, who was in the lead, stopped and beckoned Sanders forward.

"My pistol." He patted his shoulder holster. "I'll follow you. See if you notice anything from the door."

As he retraced his steps. Sanders walked across the empty hall. He paused among the jeweled pillars, uneager, whatever Ventress's instructions, to expose himself in the wide doorway with its colonnaded portico. From the center of the hall the garden and trees beyond were silent, and he turned and waited among the pillars by the alcove on his left, dozens of reflections of himself glowing in the glass-sheathed walls and furniture.

Involuntarily Sanders raised his hands to catch the rainbows of light that ran around the edges of his suit and face. A legion of El Dorados, all bearing his own features, receded in the mirrors, more images of himself as the man of light than he could have hoped for. He studied a reflection of himself in profile, noticing how the bands of color softened the drawn lines of his mouth and eyes, blurring the residue of time there that had hardened the tissues like the scales of leprosy itself. For a moment he seemed twenty years younger, the ruddy overlay of colors on his cheeks more skilful than the palette of any Rubens or Titian.

Turning his attention to the reflection facing his own, Sanders noticed with surprise that among these prismatic images of himself refracted from the sun he had found one darker twin. The profile and features were obscured, but the skin was almost ebony in color, reflecting the mottled blues and violets of the opposite end of the spectrum. Somehow menacing in this company of light, the somber figure stood motionlessly with its head turned away from him, as if aware of its negative aspect. In its lowered hand a lance of silver light flared like a star in a chalice.

Abruptly Sanders leapt behind the pillar on his left, as the Negro hiding in the alcove lunged forward across him. The knife flashed in the air past Sanders's face, its white light diving among the reflections that swerved like drunken suns around the two men, the colors bleeding off their arms and legs. Sanders kicked at the Negro's hand, half-recognizing one of the thugs he had seen on the catwalk at Port Matarre. Crouching down, his bony pointed face almost between his knees, the Negro feinted with the knife. Sanders moved back toward the staircase, and then saw the giant mulatto in the bush-shirt watching from behind a bookcase in the drawing room, a Colt automatic in his scarred hand. The frost outside had given his dark face a luminous sheen.

Before Sanders could shout up to Ventress, a shot roared out through the air over his head. Ducking down, he saw the Negro with the knife knocked to the floor, his heels kicking in pain. The punctured lattice on the wall behind him slid and shattered across a divan, and the Negro picked himself up and raced like a wounded animal through the entrance. A second shot followed him from the staircase, and Ventress moved down from his vantage point behind the banister. His tight face hidden behind the stock of the shotgun, he beckoned Sanders away from the entrance to the drawing room. The mulatto hiding by the bookcase ran across the room, firing once as he stopped below the chandelier, the impact of the explosion showering the light from the cut-glass pendants like rain over his cropped head. He shouted at a tall white-skinned man in a leather jerkin who stood by the far wall, with his back to the staircase opening a safe over the ornamental fireplace.

Covering him, the mulatto fired through the door. The man by the safe dragged a small strongbox from the upper shelf as Ventress upended the mahogany hall stand across the archway. The strongbox fell to the floor, and dozens of rubies and sapphires scattered between the tall man's feet. Ignoring Ventress, who was trying to get in a shot at the mulatto, he bent down and scooped some of the stones into his big hands. Then he and the mulatto turned and ran for the French windows, crushing aside the light frames with their shoulders.

Leaping over his barricade, Ventress entered the

drawing room, darting in and out of the overstuffed settees and armchairs. As his quarry disappeared through the trees Ventress reached the windows, then reloaded his gun with the shells in his pocket and fired a parting shot over the lawn.

He moved the barrel in Sanders's direction as the latter stepped over the hall stand into the room.

"Right, Doctor, all clear?" Ventress was breathing rapidly, his small shoulders moving about in an excess of nervous energy. "What's the matter? He didn't touch you, did he?"

Sanders went over to him. He pushed aside the gun-barrel, which Ventress still held toward him. He stared down at the bearded man's bony face and over-excited eyes.

"Ventress! You knew they were here all along—you were bloody well using me as a decoy!"

He broke off. Ventress was paying no attention to him, and was peering left and right through the French windows. Sanders turned away, a sense of limp calm coming over his fatigue. He noticed the jewels sparkling on the floor. "I thought you said Thorensen wasn't interested in gem-stones."

Ventress turned to look at Sanders, and then down at the floor below the safe. Half-dropping his shotgun, he bent over and began to touch the stones where they lay, as if puzzled to find them there. He absently pocketed a few of them, then gathered the rest together and stuffed them into his trousers.

He went back to the windows. "You're right, Sanders, of course," he said in a flat voice. "But I was thinking of your safety, believe me." Then he snapped: "Let's get out of here."

As they made their way across the lawn, Ventress lagged behind a second time. Sanders stopped, looking back at the house which loomed behind them among the trees like a giant wedding cake. Ventress was staring at the handful of gem-stones in his hand. The bright sapphires slipped between his fingers and lay on the sequined grass behind him, illuminating his footprints as he entered the dark vaults of the forest.

The summer house

For an hour they moved along the fossilized stream. Ventress remained in the lead, the shotgun held warily in front of him, his movements neat and deliberate, while Sanders limped behind. Now and then they passed a power-cruiser embedded in the crust, or a vitrified crocodile reared upwards and grimaced at them soundlessly, its mouth choked with jewels as it shifted in a fault of colored glass.

Always Ventress was on the lookout for Thorensen. Which of them was searching for the other, Sanders could not discover, nor the subject of their blood feud. Although Thorensen had twice attacked him, Ventress almost seemed to be encouraging Thorensen, deliberately exposing himself as if trying to trap the mine-owner.

"Can't we get back to Mont Royal?" Dr. Sanders shouted, his voice echoing among the vaults. "We're going deeper into the forest."

"The town is cut off, my dear Sanders. Don't worry, I'll take you there in due course." Ventress leapt nimbly over a fissure in the surface of the stream. Below the mass of dissolving crystals, a thin stream of fluid rilled down a buried channel.

Led by this white-suited figure with his preoccupied gaze, they moved on through the forest, sometimes in complete circles, as if Ventress were familiarizing himself with the topography of his jeweled twilight world. Whenever Dr. Sanders sat down to rest on one of the vitrified trunks and brushed away the crystals forming on the soles of his shoes, despite their constant movement, Ventress would wait impatiently, watching Sanders with ruminative eyes as if deciding whether to abandon him to the forest. The air was always icy, the dark shadows closing and unfolding around them.

Then, as they pressed on into the forest, leaving the stream in the hope of joining the river lower down its course, they came across the wreck of the crashed helicopter.

At first, as they passed the aircraft lying like an emblazoned fossil in a small hollow to the left of their path, Dr. Sanders failed to recognize it. Ventress stopped. With a somber expression he pointed to the huge machine, and Sanders remembered the helicopter plunging into the forest half a mile from the inspection site. The four twisted blades, veined and frosted like the wings of a giant dragonfly, had already been overgrown by the trellises of crystals hanging downwards from the near-by trees. The fuselage of the craft, partly buried in the ground, had blossomed into an enormous translucent jewel, in whose solid depths, like emblematic knights mounted in the base of a medieval ring stone, the two pilots sat frozen at their controls. Their silver helmets gave off an endless fountain of light.

"You won't help them now." A rictus of pain twisted

Ventress's mouth. Averting his face, he began to move away. "Come on, Sanders, or you'll soon be like them. The forest is changing all the time."

"Wait!" Sanders climbed over the fossilized undergrowth, kicking away pieces of the glass-like foliage. He pulled himself around the dome of the cockpit canopy. "Ventress! There's a man here!"

Together they climbed down into the floor of the hollow below the starboard side of the helicopter. Stretched out over the serpentine roots of a giant oak, across which he had been trying to drag himself, was the crystallized body of a man in military uniform. His chest and shoulders were covered by a huge cuirass of jeweled plates, the arms enclosed in the same gauntlet of annealed prisms that Sanders had seen on the man dragged from the river at Port Matarre.

"Ventress, it's the army captain! Radek!" Sanders gazed into the visor that covered the man's head, now an immense sapphire carved in the shape of a conquistador's helmet. Refracted through the prisms that had effloresced from the man's face, his features seemed to overlay one another in a dozen different planes, but Dr. Sanders could still recognize the weak-chinned face of Captain Radek, the physician in the army medical corps who had first taken him to the inspection site. He realized that Radek had gone back after all, probably searching for Sanders when he failed to emerge from the forest, and instead had found the two pilots in the helicopter.

Now rainbows glowed in the dead man's eyes.

"Ventress!" Sanders remembered the drowned man in the harbor at Port Matarre. He pressed his hands against the crystal breast-plate, trying to detect any signs of warmth within. "He's still alive inside this, help me to get him out of here!" When Ventress stood up, shaking his head over the glittering body, Sanders shouted: "Ventress, I know this man!"

Gripping his shotgun, Ventress began to climb out of the hollow. "Sanders, you're wasting your time." He shook his head, his eyes roving between the trees around them. "Leave him there, he's made his own peace."

Pushing past him, Sanders straddled the crystalline body and tried to lift it from the hollow. The weight of the body was enormous, and he could barely move one of the arms. Part of the head and shoulder, and the entire length of the right arm, had annealed themselves to the crystal outgrowths from the base of the oak. As Sanders began to kick at the winding roots, trying to free the body, Ventress shouted in warning. Wrenching at the body, Sanders managed to jerk it free. Several pieces of the crystal sheath fell from the face and shoulders.

With a cry Ventress jumped down into the hollow. He held Sanders's arm tightly. "For God's sake—!" he began, but when Sanders pushed him aside he gave up and turned away.

After a pause, his small bitter eyes watching Sanders, he stepped forward and helped him lift the jeweled body from the hollow.

A hundred yards ahead they reached the bank of the stream. The tributary had expanded into a channel some ten yards in width. In the center the fossilized crust was only a few inches thin, and they could see the running water below. Leaving Radek's glistening body on the bank, where it lay with arms outstretched, slowly deliquescing, Dr. Sanders snapped a large bough off one of the trees and began to break the crust over the water. As he drove the branch downwards the crystals fractured easily, and within a few minutes he had opened a circular aperture three or four yards wide. He dragged the branch over to the bank where Radek lay. Bending down, he lifted the body on to the branch and lashed Radek's shoulders to it with his belt. With luck the timber would support Radek's head above the water long enough for him to regain consciousness as the crystals dissolved in the moving current.

Ventress made no comment, but continued to watch Sanders with his bitter eyes. Propping his shotgun against a tree, he helped Sanders carry the body to the aperture above the water. Each holding one end of the bough, they lowered Radek feet-first into the water. The stream moved quickly and they watched the body swirl away down the white tunnel. The washed crystals on Radek's arms and legs glimmered below the water, his half-submerged head resting on the bough. Dr. Sanders limped across to the bank. He sat down on the marbled sand, picking at the sharp needles that pierced his palms and fingers. "There's a chance, that's all, but worth taking," he said. Ventress was standing a few feet away from him. "They'll be watching downriver, perhaps they'll see him."

Ventress walked up to Sanders. His small body was held stiffly, his bearded chin tucked in. The muscles of his bony face moved his mouth soundlessly, as if he were composing his reply with great care. He said: "Sanders, you were too late. One day you'll know what you took away from that man."

Dr. Sanders looked up. "What do you mean?" Irritably, he snapped: "Ventress, I owed that man something."

Ventress ignored this. "Just remember, Doctor—if you ever find me like that, *leave me*. Do you understand?"

They moved off through the forest, neither speaking to the other, Sanders sometimes falling fifty yards behind Ventress. Several times he thought Ventress had abandoned him, but always the white-suited figure, his hair and shoulders covered with a fine fur of frost, appeared into view before him. Although exasperated by Ventress's callousness and lack of sympathy for Radek, Sanders sensed that there might be some other explanation for his behavior.

At last they reached the fringes of a small clearing, bounded on three sides by the fractured dancing floor of an inlet to one side of the river. On the opposite bank a high-gabled summer house pushed its roof toward the sky through a break in the overhead canopy. From the single spire a slender web of opaque strands extended to the surrounding trees like a diaphanous veil, investing the glass garden and the crystalline summer house with a marble sheen, almost sepulchral in its intensity.

As if reinforcing this impression, the windows on to the veranda around the house were encrusted with elaborate scroll-like patterns, like the ornamented casements of a tomb.

Waving Sanders back, Ventress approached the fringes of the garden, his shotgun raised before him. For the first time since Sanders had known him, Ventress seemed uncertain of himself. He gazed across at the summer house, like an explorer venturing upon some strange and enigmatic shrine in the depths of the jungle.

High above him, its wings pinioned by the glass canopy, a golden oriole flexed slowly in the afternoon light, the ripples of its liquid aura circling outwards like the rays of a cruciform sun.

Ventress drew himself together. After waiting for any sign of movement from the summer house, he darted from tree to tree, then crossed the frozen surface of the river with a feline step. Ten yards from the summer house he stopped again, distracted by the glowing oriole in the canopy above his head.

"It's Ventress—take him!"

A shot roared into the clearing, its report echoing around the brittle foliage. Startled, Ventress crouched down on the steps of the summer house, peering up at its sealed windows. From the edge of the clearing fifty yards behind him appeared a tall blond-haired man in a black leather jerkin, the mine-owner Thorensen. Revolver in hand, he raced toward the summer house. He stopped and fired again at Ventress, the roar of the explosion reverberating around the clearing. Behind Dr. Sanders the crystal trellises of the moss suspended from the trees frosted and collapsed like the collapsing walls of a house of mirrors.

The back door of the summer house opened. A naked African, his left leg and the left side of his chest and waist covered with white surgical plaster, stepped out on to the veranda, a rifle in his hands. Moving stiffly, he leaned himself against a pillar, then fired off a shot at Ventress crouching on the steps.

Leaping down from the veranda, Ventress made off like a hare across the river, bent almost double as he darted over the faults in the surface. With a last backward glance, his thin bearded face contorted with fear, he raced toward the trees, Thorensen's burly figure lagging behind him.

Then, as Ventress reached the bend in the inlet, where it widened in its approach toward the river, the crop-headed figure of the mulatto rose from his hiding place among the sprays of swamp grass growing like silver fans from the edge of the bank. His immense black body, etched clearly against the surrounding forest by its white outline of frost, leapt forward like a bull about to gore a fleeing matador. Ventress passed within a few feet of him, and the mulatto whipped one arm and tossed a steel net through the air over Ventress's head. Knocked off balance, Ventress sidestepped and fell, then slid ten yards across the frozen surface, his startled face peering through the open mesh.

With a satisfied grunt, the mulatto pulled a long panga from his belt and lumbered forward to the small figure lying like a trussed animal in front of him. Ventress kicked at the net, trying to free the shotgun. Ten feet away, the mulatto slashed the air experimentally, then ran forward to deliver the coup de grâce.

"Thorensen! Call him back!" Sanders shouted. The rapidity with which all this had happened left Sanders standing by the edge of the clearing, his ears ringing with the explosions. He shouted again at Thorensen, who was waiting arms akimbo below the steps of the summer house. His long face was half averted, as if he preferred to take no part in this final moment.

Still lying on his back on the ground, Ventress had partly freed himself from the net. Letting go of the shotgun, he pulled the net around his waist. The mulatto towered over him, the panga raised behind his head.

With an epileptic twist, Ventress managed to move a few feet away. The mulatto roared with laughter, then let out a bellow of anger. The crystal surface had given way beneath his huge feet, and he sank up to his knees through the crust. With a heave he lifted himself on to the surface on one leg, then sank through it again as he pulled out the other. Ventress kicked the net away, and the mulatto reached forward and slashed at the ice a few inches from his heels.

Ventress stumbled to his feet. The shotgun was still entangled in the net, and he seized the bundle and ran off across the surface, sliding in and out of the half-crystallized patches. Behind him the mulatto charged like a berserk sea lion through the collapsing crust, hacking it out of his way with blows of the panga.

Ventress was out of reach. Here, where the inlet widened, the deeper channel of water running below to join the river was covered only by a thin crust. The surface frosted under Ventress's feet, but the winding lanes of firm ice held beneath his small figure. Within twenty yards he had reached the shore and darted away among the trees.

As a final shot rang out after him from the bandaged African on the veranda of the summer house, Dr. Sanders stood in the center of the clearing. He watched the mulatto wallowing in his trough of half-damp crystals, slashing at them angrily and sending up a shower of rainbowing light.

"You! Come here!" Thorensen gestured Sanders toward him with his revolver. The leather jerkin he wore over his blue suit made his large frame seem trimmer and more muscular. Below the blond hair his long face wore an expression of sullen moodiness. When Sanders approached he scrutinized him warily. "What are you doing with Ventress? Aren't you one of the visiting party? I saw you on the quay with Radek."

Dr. Sanders was about to speak when Thorensen held up his hand. With a gesture at the African on the veranda, who moved his rifle to cover Sanders, Thorensen walked off in the direction of the mulatto. "I'll see you in a minute—don't try to run for it."

The mulatto had climbed up on to the firmer surface near the summer house. As Thorensen approached he began to gesticulate and shout, waving his panga at the broken surface as if trying to cover up his failure to catch Ventress. Thorensen nodded, then dismissed him with a bored wave. Walking forward across the surface, he began to test the half-formed crystals with his feet. For several minutes he paced up and down, gazing in the direction of the river, as if marking out the dimensions of the subterranean channels.

He returned to Sanders, the damp crystals on his shoes giving off glimmers of colored light. He listened in a distracted way as Sanders explained how he had been trapped in the forest after the crash of the helicopter. Sanders described his accidental meeting with Ventress and, subsequently, the discovery of Radek's body. Remembering Ventress's bitter protests at the time, Sanders stressed his reasons for this apparent attempt to drown a dead man.

Thorensen nodded dourly. "Maybe he has a chance." As if to reassure Sanders, he added: "You did the right thing."

The mulatto and the naked African half-swathed in surgical tape were sitting on the steps of the veranda. The mulatto was honing his panga, while the other rested his rifle on his one bare knee, scanning the forest. He had the slim intelligent face of a young clerk or junior foreman, and now and then glanced at Sanders with the look of a man who recognized another member, however remote, of the same educated caste. Sanders remembered him as the knife-wielding attacker whose dark reflection he had confused with his own in the hall of mirrors at Thorensen's house.

Thorensen was gazing over one shoulder at the windows of the summer house, only half-aware of Sanders standing beside him. Sanders noticed that, unlike Ventress's suit and his own clothes, Thorensen's leather jerkin was unaffected by the frost. "Can you take me back to the army post?" he asked Thorensen. "I've been trying to get out of the forest for hours. Do you know the Bourbon Hotel?"

A morose frown twisted Thorensen's long face. "The army's a long way off. The freeze is spreading all through the forest." He pointed across the river with his revolver. "What about Ventress? The bearded man. Where did you meet him?"

Sanders explained himself again. Neither Thorensen nor the mulatto recognized him as Ventress's defender during the attack at Port Matarre. "He was taking shelter in a house near the river. Your house, he said. Why were you shooting at him? Is he some sort of criminal—trying to steal from your mine?"

There was a laugh at this from the young African with the rifle. Thorensen nodded without expression. His manner was furtive and shifty, as if unsure of himself and what to do with Sanders. "Worse than that. He's a madman, completely crazy."

He turned and started to walk up the steps, waving to Sanders as if prepared to let him make his own way into the forest. "You'd better be careful, there's no knowing what the forest is going to do. Keep moving, but circle around on yourself."

"Wait a minute!" Sanders called after him. "I want to rest here. I need a map, I've got to find this Bourbon Hotel."

"A map? What good is a map now?" Thorensen hesitated, glancing up at the summer house as if worried that Sanders might in some way defile its luminous whiteness. As the doctor's arms fell limply to his sides

Thorensen shrugged and beckoned his two men to follow him.

"Thorensen!" Sanders stepped forward. He pointed to the young African with the bandaged leg, "Let me look at his dressing and make him more comfortable. I'm a doctor."

The three men on the veranda turned together, even the big mulatto watching Sanders with interest. A note of calculation crossed his bilious eyes. Thorensen was looking down at Sanders as if recognizing him for the first time.

"A doctor? Yes, Radek said—I remember. All right, Doctor—?"

"Sanders. I've nothing with me, no drugs or—"

"That's O.K., Doctor," Thorensen said. "That's good, in fact." He nodded to himself, as if still uncertain to invite Sanders into the summer house. Then he relented. "Right, Doctor, you can come in for five minutes. I might want to ask you for something."

Dr. Sanders climbed the steps onto the veranda. The summer house consisted of a single circular room and a small kitchen and store at the rear. Heavy shutters had been placed over the windows, now locked to the casements by the interstitial crystals, and the only light entered through the door.

Thorensen glanced around at the forest and then holstered his pistol. As the two Africans made their way round to the back Thorensen turned the door handle. Through the frosted panes Dr. Sanders saw the dim outlines of a high four-poster bed, obviously that removed from the bedroom in the mansion where he and

Ventress had sheltered from the storm. Gilded cupids played about the mahogany canopy, pipes to their lips, and four naked caryatids with upraised arms formed the corner posts.

Thorensen cleared his throat. "Mrs.—Ventress," he explained at last in a low voice.

Serena

They gazed down at the occupant of the bed, who lay back on a large satin bolster, a febrile hand on the silk counterpane. At first Dr. Sanders thought he was looking at an elderly woman, probably Ventress's mother, and then realized that in fact she was little more than a child, a young woman in her early twenties. Her long platinum hair lay in a white shawl over her shoulders, her thin high-cheeked face raised to the scanty light. Once she might have had a nervous porcelain beauty, but her wasted skin and the fading glow of light in her half-closed eyes gave her the appearance of someone preternaturally aged, reminding Dr. Sanders of his patients in the children's ward at the hospital near the *léproserie* in the last minutes before their death.

"Thorensen." Her voice cracked in the amber gloom. "It's getting cold again. Can't you light a fire?"

"The wood won't burn, Serena. It's all turned into glass." Thorensen stood at the foot of the bed, peering down at the young woman. In his leather jacket he looked like a policeman uneasily on duty in a sick-room. He unzipped the jacket. "I brought these for you, Serena, they'll help you."

He leaned forward, hiding something from Dr.

Sanders, and then spilled several handfuls of red and blue gem-stones across the counterpane. Rubies and sapphires of many sizes, they glittered in the thinning afternoon light with a fevered power.

"Thorensen, thank you—" The girl's free hand scuttled across the counterpane to the stones. Her child-like face had become almost vulpine with greed. An expression of surprising craftiness came into her eyes, and Sanders sensed why the burly mine-owner treated her with such deference. Seizing a handful of the jewels, she brought them up to her neck and pressed them tightly against her skin, where the bruises formed like fingerprints. Their contact seemed to revive her and she stirred her legs, several of the jewels slipping to the floor. She gazed up at Dr. Sanders, and then turned to Thorensen.

"What were you shooting at?" she asked after an interval. "There was a gun going off. It gave me a headache."

"Just a crocodile, Serena. There are some smart crocodiles around here. I have to watch them."

The young woman nodded. With a hand still clutching the jewels she pointed at Sanders. "Who's he? What's he doing here?"

"He's a doctor, Serena. Captain Radek sent him, he's all right."

"But you said I didn't need any doctors."

"You don't, Serena, I know that. Dr. Sanders here was just looking by, to see one of the men." During this labored catechism Thorensen kneaded the lapels of his jacket, looking everywhere around the room but at Serena.

Sanders moved closer to the bed, assuming that Thorensen would now let him examine the young woman. Her tubercular breathing and severe anemia needed little further diagnosis, but he reached forward to take her wrist.

"Doctor—" On some kind of confused impulse Thorensen pulled him back from the bed. He made an uncertain gesture with one hand, then waved Sanders toward the kitchen door. "I think later, Doctor—right?" He turned quickly to the young woman. "You get some rest now, Serena."

"But, Thorensen, I need more of these, you only brought me a few today—" Her hand, like a claw, searched the counterpane for the jewels, the handfuls that Thorensen and the mulatto had taken from the wall-safe earlier that afternoon.

Sanders was about to protest, but the young woman turned away from them and seemed to subside into sleep, the jewels lying like scarabs on the white skin of her breast.

Thorensen nudged Sanders with his elbow. They stepped into the kitchen. Before he closed the door Thorensen looked down at the young woman with wistful eyes, as if frightened that she might dissolve into dust if he left her.

Only half-aware of Sanders, he said: "We'll have something to eat."

At the far end of the kitchen, by the door, the mulatto and the naked African sat on a bench, half-asleep over their weapons. The kitchen was almost empty. A disconnected refrigerator stood on the cold stove. Thorensen opened the door and began to empty the remainder of the jewels from his pockets on to the shelves, where they lay like cherries among the half-dozen cans of corned beef and beans. A light glacé frost covered the enamel exterior of the refrigerator, as everything else in the kitchen, but the inner walls of the cabinet remained unaffected.

"Who is she?" Dr. Sanders asked as Thorenson prised the lid off a can. "You've got to get her away from here. She needs careful treatment, this is no place for—"

"Doctor!" Thorensen raised a hand to silence Sanders. He seemed always to be concealing something, his eyes fractionally lowered below Sanders's. "She's my—wife, now," he said with curious emphasis, as if still trying to establish the fact in his mind. "Serena. She's safer here, as long as I watch out for Ventress."

"But he's only trying to save her! For God's sake, man—"

"He's insane!" Thorensen shouted with sudden force. The two Negroes at the other end of the kitchen turned to look at him. "He spent six months in a strait jacket! He isn't trying to help Serena, he just wants to take her back to his crazy house in the middle of the swamp."

As they ate, forking the cold meat straight from the can, he told Sanders something of Ventress, this strange and melancholy architect, who had designed many of the new government buildings in Lagos and Accra, and then two years earlier abruptly abandoned his work in disgust. He had married Serena when she was seventeen, after bribing her parents, a poor French colonial couple in Libreville, within a few hours of seeing her in the street outside his office as he left it for the last time. He had then carried her away to a grotesque folly he had built on a water-logged island among the crocodiles in the swamps ten miles to the north of Mont Royal, where the Matarre River expanded into a series of shallow lakes. According to Thorensen, Ventress had rarely spoken to Serena after the marriage, and prevented her from leaving the house or seeing anyone except a blind Negro servant. Apparently he saw his young bride in a sort of pre-Raphaelite dream, caged within his house like the lost spirit of his imagination. Thorensen had found her there, already tubercular, on one of his hunting trips, when his power-cruiser had broken its propeller shaft and was beached on the island. He visited her several times during Ventress's long absences, and she finally escaped with him after the house had caught fire. Thorensen sent her off to a sanatorium in Rhodesia, and his own great mansion at Mont Royal, filled with its imitation antiques, had been prepared for her homecoming. After her disappearance and the first moves toward the annulment of the marriage, Ventress had gone berserk and spent some time as a voluntary patient at an asylum. Now he had returned with the single-minded ambition of abducting Serena and taking her off once more to his ruined house in the swamps. Thorensen seemed convinced that Ventress's morbid and lunatic presence was responsible for Serena's lingering malaise.

However, when Sanders asked to see her again, in the hope that he would be able to persuade Thorensen to remove her from the frozen forest, the mine-owner demurred.

"She's all right here," he told Sanders doggedly. "Don't worry."

"But, Thorensen, how much longer do you think she'll last here? The whole forest is crystallizing, don't you realize—?"

"She's all right!" Thorensen insisted. He stood up and looked down at the table, his stooped figure with its blond hair like a gallows in the dusk. "Doctor, I've been in this forest a long time. The only chance she has is here."

Puzzled by this cryptic remark, and whatever private meaning it had for Thorensen, Sanders sat down at a chair by the table. A siren sounded in the dusk from the direction of the river, its echoes reflected off the brittle foliage around the summer house.

Thorensen spoke to the mulatto and came back to Sanders.

"I'll leave you in their hands, Doctor. I'll be back in a short while." He took a roll of surgical tape from the shelf beside the cooker, and then beckoned to the injured African. "Kagwa, let the Doctor look at you."

After Thorensen had gone Sanders examined the shot-wounds in the African's leg and chest, and cleaned the rough lint pads. A dozen pellets had penetrated the man's skin, but the wounds already seemed half healed, inert punctures that showed no tendency to bleed or fester.

"You're lucky," he told the African when he had finished. "I'm surprised you can walk at all." He added: "I saw you this afternoon—in the mirrors at Thorensen's house." The youth smiled amicably. "It was Monsieur Ventress we were looking for, Doctor. There's much hunting in this forest, eh?"

"You're right—though I doubt if any of you really know what you're after." Sanders noticed the mulatto was watching him with more than usual interest. "Tell me," he asked Kagwa, deciding to make the most of the young man's easy-going manner, "do you work for Thorensen? At his mine?"

"The mine is closed, Doctor, but I was number one in charge of technical stores." He nodded with some pride. "For the whole mine."

"An important job." Sanders pointed toward the bedroom door, beyond which the young woman lay. "Mrs. Ventress—Serena, I think Thorensen called her. She's got to be moved from here. You're an intelligent man, Mr. Kagwa, you realize that. A few more days here and she'll be as good as dead."

Kagwa turned away from the doctor and smiled to himself. He looked down at the bandages on his leg and chest and touched them wistfully. " 'Good as dead'—a fascinating phrase, Doctor. I understand what you say, but it's best now for Madame Ventress to stay here."

Barely controlling his voice, Sanders said: "For God's sake, Kagwa, she'll *die!* Haven't you grasped that? What on earth is Thorensen playing at?" Kagwa raised his hands to restrain Sanders. Turning on his strong leg, he leaned the other against the table. "*You* are speaking,

Doctor, in medical terms. Listen!" he insisted when Sanders tried to remonstrate. "I am not giving you any ju-ju magic, I am an educated African. But many strange things happen in this forest, Doctor, you will—"

He broke off as the mulatto barked something at him and went out onto the veranda. They could hear Thorensen approaching with two or three men, their boots crushing the brittle foliage along the bank.

As Sanders moved toward the door Kagwa touched his arm. A warning smile held the doctor's attention. "Remember, Doctor, walk one way through the forest, but look two ways—" Then, rifle in hand, he limped off on his white leg.

Thorensen greeted Sanders on the veranda. He clumped up the steps, zipping up his leather jacket in the tomb-like coldness of the summer house.

"Still here, Doctor? I've got a couple of guides for you." He pointed to the two Africans who stood at the bottom of the steps. Members of the crew of his motor-cruiser, they wore jeans and blue denim shirts. One had a white peaked cap pulled down across his forehead. Both carried carbines and were scanning the forest with marked interest. "My boat is moored near here," Thorensen explained, "I'd send you back by river if the engine hadn't seized up. Anyway, they'll get you to Mont Royal in no time."

With this he strode off into the kitchen, and a moment later Sanders heard him enter the bedroom.

Surrounded by the glistening figures of the four Africans, etched in hoar frost against the darkness, Sanders waited for Thorensen to reappear. Then he turned and followed his guides, leaving Thorensen and Serena Ventress barricaded together in the sepulchre of the summer house. As they entered the forest he looked back at the veranda, where the young African, Kagwa, was still watching him. His dark body, almost exactly bisected by the white bandages, reminded Sanders of Louise Peret and her references to the day of the equinox. Thinking over his brief conversation with Kagwa, he began to realize Thorensen's motives for trying to keep Serena Ventress within the affected zone. Fearing that she might die, he preferred this half-animate immolation within the crystal vaults to her physical death in the world outside. Perhaps he had seen insects and birds pinioned alive inside their prisms, and misguidedly decided that this offered the one means of escape for his dying bride.

Following a path that skirted the inlet, they set off toward the inspection site, which Sanders estimated to be some three-quarters of a mile down-river. With luck an army unit would be stationed at the nearest margins of the affected zone, and the soldiers would be able to retrace his steps and rescue the mine-owner and Serena Ventress.

The two guides moved along at a rapid pace, barely pausing to choose their direction, one in front of Sanders and the other, wearing the peaked cap, ten yards behind. After fifteen minutes, when they had covered very nearly a mile and yet were still within the main body of the forest, Sanders realized that the sailors' real task was not to guide him to safety at all. In turning him out into the forest Thorensen was no doubt using him, in Ventress's phrase, as a decoy, confident that the architect would try to reach Sanders for news of his abducted wife.

When, for the second time, they entered a small glade between two groups of forest oaks Sanders stopped and walked back to the sailor in the peaked cap. He started to remonstrate with him, but the man shook his head and beckoned Sanders on with his carbine.

Five minutes later Sanders found that he was alone. The pathway ahead was deserted. He made his way back to the glade, where the shadows shone emptily on the forest floor. The guides had disappeared into the undergrowth.

Sanders glanced over his shoulder at the dark grottoes around the glade, listening for any footsteps, but the sheaths of the trees sang and crackled as the forest cooled in the darkness. Above, through the lattices that stretched across the glade, he could see the fractured bowl of the moon. Around him, in the vitreous walls, the reflected stars glittered like fire-flies.

He pressed on along the path. His clothes had begun to glow in the dark, the frost that covered his suit spangled by the starlight. Spurs of crystal grew from the dial of his wrist-watch, imprisoning the hands within a medallion of moonstone.

A hundred yards behind him the roar of a shotgun drummed through the trees. A carbine fired twice in reply, and a confused medley of running feet, shouts and gunfire reached Sanders as he crouched behind a trunk.

Abruptly everything fell quiet again. Sanders waited, searching the darkness around him. A few fragmentary, half-formed noises came down the pathway. There was a brief shout, cut off by a second blast from the shotgun. As if far away, an African's voice cried plaintively.

Sanders made his way back through the trees. Five yards from the path, in a hollow among the roots of an oak, he found the dying figure of one of his guides. The man half-sat against the trunk, knocked back across the roots by the force of the gunblast. He watched Sanders approach with vague eyes, one hand touching the blood that ran from his shattered chest. Ten feet away lay his peaked cap, the imprint of a small foot stamped into its crown.

Sanders knelt down beside him. The African looked away. His wet eyes were staring through an interval in the trees at the distant river. Its petrified surface stretched like white ice to the jeweled forest on the opposite shore.

A siren sounded from the direction of the summer house. Realizing that Thorensen and his men would make short work of him, Sanders stood up. The African was dying quietly at his feet. Leaving him, Sanders crossed the path and set off toward the river.

When he reached the bank he could see the motor-cruiser moored in a pool of clear water a quarter of a mile away, at the mouth of a small creek that wound off past a ruined jetty. A searchlight shone from the bridge, playing on the white surface that swept past the open water down the channel of the river.

Crouching down, Sanders ducked in and out of the

grass growing from the edges of the bank. His running shadow, illuminated by the sweeping searchlight, flickered ahead of him among the vitrified trees, the dark image speckled by the jeweled light.

Half a mile down-river the channel had widened into a broad glacier. Across the surface Sanders could see the distant roof-tops of Mont Royal. Like a causeway of frozen gas, it flowed on through the darkness, riven by deep faults. At its bottom ran the icy water of the original channel. Sanders peered over the edges of the fissures, hoping for some sign of Captain Radek's body stranded on the beaches of ice below.

Forced to leave the river, when the surface broke up into a succession of giant cataracts, he approached the outskirts of Mont Royal. The frosted outline of the picket fence and the debris of military equipment marked the site of the former inspection area. The laboratory trailer, and the tables and equipment near by, had been enveloped by the intense frost. The branches in the centrifuge had blossomed again into brilliant jeweled sprays. Sanders picked up a discarded helmet, now a glass porcupine, and drove it through a window of the trailer.

In the darkness the white-roofed houses of the mining town gleamed like the funerary temples of a necropolis. Their cornices were ornamented with countless spires and gargoyles, linked together across the roads by the expanding tracery. A frozen wind moved through the deserted streets, waist-high forests of fossil spurs, the abandoned cars embedded within them like armored saurians on an ancient ocean floor.

Everywhere the process of transformation was accelerating. Sanders's feet were encased in huge crystal slippers. These spurs enabled him to walk along the sharp edges of the roadway, but soon the opposing needles would fuse together and lock him to the ground.

The eastern entrance to the town was sealed by the forest and the erupting roadway. Sanders limped back to the river, hoping to climb the series of cataracts and make his way back to the base camp to the south. As he scaled the first of the crystal blocks he could hear the underground streams beneath the moraine sluicing away into the open river.

A long crevice with an overhanging sill ran diagonally across the cataract, and led him into a series of galleries like the aerial terraces of a cathedral. Beyond these the icefalls spilled away onto a white beach that seemed to mark the southern limits of the affected zone. The vents of the buried channels lay among the icefalls, and a clear stream of moonlit water ran between the blocks and opened into a shallow river, at least ten feet below the original course. Sanders walked along the frozen beach, looking at the vitrified forest on either side. Already the trees were duller, the crystal sheaths lying in patches against the sides of the trunk like half-melted ice.

Fifty yards along the ice beach, which narrowed as the water swept past it, Sanders saw a man's dark figure standing beneath one of the overhanging trees. With a tired wave, Sanders began to run toward him.

"Wait!" he called, afraid that the man might sidestep into the forest. "Over here—"

Ten yards from him Sanders slowed to a walk. The man had not moved from beneath the tree. Head down, he was carrying a large piece of driftwood across his shoulders—a soldier, Sanders decided, foraging for firewood.

As Sanders drew up to him, the man stepped forward, in a gesture that was at once defensive and aggressive. The light from the icefalls illuminated his ravaged body.

"Radek—good God!" Appalled, Sanders stumbled back, almost tripping over a half-exposed root in the ice. "Radek—?"

The man hesitated, like a wounded animal uncertain whether to surrender or attack. Across his shoulders he still carried the wooden yoke which Sanders had fastened there. The left side of his body gave a painful heave, as if he were trying to throw off this incubus, but he was unable to raise his hands to the buckle behind his head. The right side of his body seemed to hang loosely, suspended from the wooden cross-tree like a long-dead corpse. A huge wound had been torn across the shoulder, the flesh bared to the elbow and sternum. The raw face, from which a single eye gazed at Sanders, still ran with blood that fell to the white ice below.

Recognizing the belt with which he had fastened the wooden spar to Radek's shoulders, Dr. Sanders moved forward, gesturing to the man as if to pacify him. He remembered Ventress's warning, and the pieces of crystal that he had torn away from the body when he dragged Radek from the helicopter. Then, too, he remembered Aragon tapping his eye-tooth and saying "Covered—? My tooth is the whole gold, Doctor."

"Radek, let me help—" Sanders edged forward as Radek hesitated. "Believe me, I wanted to save you—"

Still trying to shift the wooden spar from his shoulders, Radek gazed down at Sanders. Unformed thoughts seemed to cross his face, and then the one blinking eye came into focus.

"Radek—" Sanders raised a hand to restrain him, unsure whether Radek would charge him or bolt like a wounded beast into the forest.

With a shambling step, Radek drew nearer. A grunt-like noise came from his throat. He moved again, almost toppled by the swinging spar.

"Take me—" he began. There was another lurching stride. He held out a bloody arm like a scepter. "Take me *back!*"

He struggled on, the heavy spar swinging his shoulders from left to right, one foot flapping on to the ice, his face lit by the jeweled light from the forest. Sanders watched him as he jerked forward, the arm held out as if to clasp Sanders's shoulder. Already, however, he seemed to have forgotten Sanders, his attention fixed on the light from the icefalls.

Sanders moved out of his way, ready to let him go by. With a sudden sidestep Radek swung the wooden beam and drove Sanders in front of him. "*Take me—!*"

"Radek—!" Winded by the blow, Sanders stumbled ahead, like an onlooker driven towards some bloody Golgotha by its intended victim. One lurching stride after another, his pace quickening as the prismatic light of the forest mingled again with his blood, Radek pressed on, the beam across his shoulders cutting off Sanders's escape.

Sanders ran towards the icefalls. Twenty yards from the first of the blocks, where the clear streams of the subterranean channels ran across his feet, as dark and cool as his memories of the world beyond, he turned and raced down into the shallows. Radek let out his stricken cry for the last time, and Sanders plunged to his shoulders into the river and swam away across the silver water.

The
mask

Some hours later, as he walked dripping through the edges of the illuminated forest, Sanders came to a wide road deserted in the moonlight. In the distance he saw the outlines of a white hotel. With its long façade and tumbled columns it looked like a floodlit ruin. To the left of the road, the forest slopes moved upwards to the blue hills above Mont Royal.

This time, as he approached the man standing beside a Land-Rover in the empty forecourt of the hotel, his wave was answered by a ready shout. A second figure patrolling the ruined hotel ran across the drive. A search-light on the roof of the car was played on to the road in front of Dr. Sanders. The two natives, wearing the uniform of the local hospital service, came forward to meet him. In the light from the forest their liquid eyes watched Dr. Sanders as they helped him into the car, their dark fingers feeling at the drenched fabric of his suit.

Dr. Sanders sat back, too tired to identify himself to the men. One of them climbed into the driving-seat and switched on the car's radio transmitter. As he spoke into the microphone his eyes stared at the crystals still dissolving on Dr. Sanders's shoes and wristwatch. The white light sparkled faintly in the dark cabin. The last of the crystals on the dial of the wristwatch gave out their light and faded, and with a sudden movement the hands began to turn.

The road marked the final boundary of the affected zone, and to Dr. Sanders the darkness around him seemed absolute, the black air inert and empty. After the endless glimmer of the vitrified forest the trees along the road, the ruined hotel and even the two men with him appeared to be shadowy images of themselves, replicas of illuminated originals in some distant land at the source of the petrified river. Despite his relief at escaping from the forest, this feeling of flatness and unreality, of being in the slack shallows of a spent world, filled Sanders with a sense of failure and disappointment.

A car approached along the road. The driver signalled with the searchlight on the Land-Rover and the car turned and came to a halt beside them. A tall man wearing an army battledress over his civilian clothes jumped out. He peered through the window at Sanders, and then nodded at the native driver.

"Dr. Sanders—?" he asked. "Are you all right?"

"Aragon!" Sanders opened his door and started to get out, but Aragon motioned him back. "Captain—I'd almost forgotten. Is Louise with you? Mademoiselle Peret?"

Aragon shook his head. "She's with the other visitors at the camp, Doctor. We thought you might come out this way, I've been watching the road." Aragon moved aside, so that the light from his car's headlamps showed more of Sanders's face. He looked into Sanders's eyes, as if trying to assess the inner impact of the forest. "You're lucky to be here, Doctor. Many of the soldiers are feared lost in the forest—they think Captain Radek is dead. The affected area is spreading out in all directions. It's many times the previous size."

The driver in Aragon's car cut his engine. As the headlamps faded Sanders sat forward. "Louise—she's safe—Captain? I'd like to see her."

"Tomorrow, Doctor. She will come to your friends' clinic. You must see them first, she understands that. Dr. Clair and his wife are at the clinic now. They will look after you."

He went back to his car. It turned and made off at speed down the dark road.

Five minutes later, after a short drive down a side turning past an old mine-works, the Land-Rover entered the compound of the mission hospital. A few oil lamps burned in the outbuildings, and several native families huddled by their carts in the yard, reluctant to take shelter indoors. The men sat in a group by the empty fountain in the center, the smoke from their cheroots forming white plumes in the darkness.

"Is Dr. Clair here?" Sanders asked the driver. "And Mrs. Clair?"

"They both here, sir." The driver glanced across at Sanders, still unsure of this apparition that had materialized from the crystalline forest. "You Dr. Sanders, sir?" he ventured as they parked.

"That's it. They're expecting me?"

"Yes, sir. Dr. Clair in Mont Royal yesterday for you, but trouble in the town, sir, he go away."

"I know. Everything went crazy—I'm sorry I missed him."

As Sanders climbed out of the car a familiar rotund figure in a white cotton jacket, short-sighted eyes below a domed forehead, hurried down the steps toward him.

"Edward—? My dear chap, for heaven's sake—!" He took Sanders's arm. "Where on earth have you been?"

Sanders felt himself relaxing for the first time since his arrival at Port Matarre, indeed, since his departure from the *léproserie* at Fort Isabelle. "Max, I wish I knew—it's good to see you." He shook Clair's hand, holding it in a tight grip. "It's been insane here—how are you, Max? And how's Suzanne?—is she—?"

"She's fine, fine. Hold on a moment." Leaving Sanders on the steps, Clair went back to the native drivers by the Land-Rover and patted each of them on the shoulder. He looked around at the other natives in the compound, waving to them as they squatted on their bundles in the dim light of the flares. Half a mile away, beyond the roofs of the outbuildings, an immense pall of silver light glowed in the night sky above the forest.

"Suzanne will be thrilled to see you, Edward," Max said as he rejoined Sanders. He seemed more preoccupied than Sanders had remembered him. "We've talked about you a lot—I'm sorry about yesterday afternoon. Suzanne had promised to visit one of the mine dispensaries, when Thorensen contacted me we got our lines crossed." The excuse was a palpably lame one, and Max smiled apologetically.

They entered an inner courtyard and walked across to a long chalet at the far end. Sanders stopped, glancing through the windows of the empty wards. Somewhere a generator hummed, and a few electric light bulbs glowed at the ends of corridors, but the hospital seemed deserted.

"Max—I made an appalling blunder." Sanders spoke rapidly, hoping that Suzanne would not appear and interrupt him. Half an hour from then, as the three of them relaxed over their drinks in the comfort of the Clairs' lounge, Radek's tragedy would cease to seem real. "This man Radek—a captain in the medical corps—I found him in the center of the forest, completely crystallized. You know what I mean?" Max nodded, his eyes looking Sanders up and down with a more than usually watchful gaze. Sanders went on: "I thought the only way of saving him was to immerse him in the river—but I had to tear him loose! Some of the crystals came off, I didn't realize—"

"Edward!" Max took his arm and tried to steer him along the path. "There's no—"

Sanders pushed his hand away. "Max, I found him later, I'd torn half his face and chest away—!"

"For God's sake!" Max clenched his fist. "Yours wasn't the first mistake, don't reproach yourself!"

"Max, I don't—understand me, it wasn't just that!" Sanders hesitated. "The point is—he wanted to go *back!* He wanted to go back into the forest and be crystallized again! He knew, Max, he *knew!*"

Lowering his head, Clair moved away a few paces. He glanced at the darkened French windows of the chalet, where the tall figure of his wife watched them from the half-opened door. "Suzanne's there," he said. "She's pleased to see you, Edward, but—" Almost vaguely, as if distracted by matters other than those which Sanders had described, he added: "You'll want a change of clothes, I have a suit that will fit you—one of the European patients, deceased, if you don't mind that—and something to eat. It's damned cold in the forest."

Sanders was looking at Suzanne Clair. Instead of coming forward to greet him, she had retreated into the darkness of the lounge, and at first Sanders wondered whether some residue of their old embarrassment still remained. Although Sanders felt that his past affair with Suzanne if anything bound Max and himself together far more than it separated them, Max seemed distant and nervous, almost as if he resented Sanders's arrival.

But Sanders could see the smile of greeting on Suzanne's face. She was wearing a night robe of black silk that made her tall figure seem almost invisible against the shadows in the lounge, the pale lantern of her face floating like a nimbus above it.

"Suzanne—it's wonderful to see you." Sanders took her hand with a laugh. "I was frightened you might both have been swallowed by the forest. How are you?"

"Very happy, Edward." Still holding Sanders's arm, Suzanne turned to face her husband. "Delighted that you've come, you'll be able to share the forest with us now."

"My dear, I think the poor man has had more than his fair share already." Max bent down behind the sofa against the bookshelf and switched on the desk lamp that had been placed on the floor. The dim light illuminated the gold lettering on the leather spines of his books, but the rest of the room remained in darkness. "Do you realize that he's been trapped in the forest since late yesterday afternoon?"

"Trapped—?" Turning away from Sanders, Suzanne went over to the French windows and closed the door. She looked out at the brilliant night sky over the forest, and then sat down in a chair near the blackwood cabinet against the far wall. "Is that quite the word to use? I envy you, Edward, it must have been a wonderful experience."

"Well—" Accepting a drink from Max, who was now half-filling his own glass from the whisky decanter, Sanders leaned against the mantelpiece. Hidden in the shadows by the cabinet, Suzanne was still smiling at him, but this reflection of her former good humor seemed overlaid by the ambiguous atmosphere in the lounge. He wondered whether this was due to his own fatigue, but there seemed something out of key in their meeting, as if some unseen dimension had been let obliquely into the room. He was still wearing the clothes in which he had swum the river, but Max made no move toward helping him to change.

Sanders raised his glass to Suzanne. "I suppose one could call it wonderful," he said. "It's a matter of degree —I was unprepared for everything here."

"How marvelous—you'll never forget it." Suzanne sat forward. She wore her long black hair in an unusual manner, well forward over her face, so that it concealed her cheeks. "Tell me about it all, Edward, I—"

"My dear." Max held up his hand. "Give the poor man time to catch his breath. Besides, he'll want a meal now, and then to get to bed. We can discuss it all over breakfast." To Sanders he explained: "Suzanne spends a lot of time wandering through the forest."

"Wandering—?" Sanders repeated. "What do you mean?"

"Only through the fringes, Edward," Suzanne said. "We're on the edge of the forest here, but there's enough—I've seen those jeweled vaults." With animation, she said: "A few mornings ago when I went out before dawn my slippers were beginning to crystallize— my feet were turning into diamonds and emeralds!"

With a smile, Max said: "My dear, you're the princess in the enchanted wood."

"Max, I *was*—" Suzanne nodded, her eyes gazing at her husband as he looked down at the carpet. She turned to Sanders, "Edward, we could never leave here now."

Sanders shrugged. "I understand, Suzanne, but you may have to. The affected area is spreading. God only knows what the source of all this is, but there doesn't seem much prospect of stopping it."

"Why try?" Suzanne looked up at Sanders. "Shouldn't we be grateful to the forest for giving us such a bounty?"

Max finished his drink. "Suzanne, you're moralizing like some missionary. All Edward wants at this moment is a change of clothes and a meal." He went over to the door. "I'll be with you in a moment, Edward. There's a room ready for you. Help yourself to another drink."

When he had gone, Sanders said to Suzanne, as he

filled his glass with soda: "You must be tired. I'm sorry to have kept you up."

"Not at all. I sleep during the day now—Max, and I decided we should keep the dispensary open round the clock." Aware that the explanation was not wholly convincing, she added: "To be frank, I prefer the night. One can see the forest better."

"That's true. You're not frightened of it, Suzanne?"

"Why should I be? It's so easy to be more frightened of one's feelings than of the things that prompt them. The forest isn't like that—I've accepted it, and all the fears that go with them." In a quieter voice, she added: "I'm glad you're here, Edward. I'm afraid Max doesn't understand what's happening in the forest—I mean in the widest sense—to all our ideas of time and mortality. How can I put it? 'Life, like a dome of many-colored glass, stains the white radiance of eternity.' I'm sure you understand."

Carrying his glass, Sanders walked across the darkened room. Although his eyes had become accustomed to the dim light, Suzanne's face still remained hidden in the shadows behind the blackwood cabinet. The faintly quizzical smile that had hovered about her mouth since his arrival was still there, almost beckoning to him.

As he drew closer to her, he realized that this slight upward inclination of the mouth was not a smile at all, but a facial rictus caused by the nodular thickening of the upper lip. The skin of her face had a characteristic dusky appearance, which she had managed to hide by her long hair and a lavish use of powder. Despite this camouflage, he could see the nodular lumps all over her face and in the lobe of her left ear as she drew back fractionally in her chair, raising her shoulder. Already, after his years of experience at the leper hospital, he recognized the beginnings of the so-called leonine mask.

Confused by this discovery, although he had half-anticipated it since Suzanne's first letter to him from Mont Royal, Sanders moved away across the room, hoping Suzanne had failed to notice the telltale way in which he had spilt some of his drink on to the carpet. His first feelings of anger at this crime of nature against someone who had already spent much of her own life trying to cure others of the disease, gave way to a sense of relief, as if this particular disaster were one for which both of them were psychologically well prepared. He realized that he had been waiting for Suzanne to catch the disease, that for him this had probably been her one valid role. Even their affair had been an unconscious attempt to bring about this very end. It was himself, and not the poor devils in the *léproserie*, who had been the real source of infection for Suzanne.

Sanders finished his drink and put it down, then turned to face Suzanne. Despite their previous closeness, he found it almost impossible to express himself to her. After a pause, he said lamely: "I was sorry you left Fort Isabelle at the time, Suzanne. In fact, it was an effort to stop myself following you straightaway. I'm glad you came, though. It may seem a strange choice to some people, but I understand. Who could blame you for trying to escape from the dark side of the sun?"

Suzanne shook her head, either puzzled by this cryptic

reference or preferring not to understand it. "What do you mean?"

Sanders hesitated. Although she appeared to be smiling, Suzanne was in fact trying to control this involuntary movement of her mouth. Her once elegant face was twisted by a barely concealed scowl.

He gestured. "I was thinking of our patients at Fort Isabelle. For them—"

"It's nothing to do with them. Edward, you're tired, and I have to be at the dispensary. I mustn't keep your supper any longer." With a brisk movement, Suzanne stood up, her slim figure taller than Sanders. Her powdered face looked down at him with the skull-like intensity he remembered in Ventress. Then once again the deformed smile supervened.

"Good night, Edward. We'll see you at breakfast, you have so much to tell us."

Sanders stopped her at the door. "Suzanne—"

"What is it, Edward?" She half-closed the door, shutting out the light from the corridor that cut across her face.

Sanders fumbled for something to say, and in a kind of half-remembered reflex raised his arms to embrace her. Then, as much attracted as repelled by her injured face, but knowing that he must first understand his own motives, he turned away.

"There's nothing to tell you, Suzanne," he said. "You've seen everything here in the forest."

"Not everything, Edward," Suzanne told him. "One day you must take me there."

The white hotel

The next morning, wearing the dead man's clothes, Sanders met Louise Peret. He had spent the night in one of the four empty chalets that formed the sides of a small courtyard behind the Clairs' bungalow. The remainder of the European medical staff had left the hospital, and before breakfast Sanders wandered through the deserted chalets, trying to prepare himself for the coming meeting with Suzanne. The few books and magazines left behind on the shelves and the unused cans in the kitchen were like the residue of a distant world.

His new suit had been the property of a Belgian engineer at one of the mines. The man, roughly his own age, he assumed from the cut of the trousers and jacket, had died some weeks earlier of pneumonia. In the pockets of the jacket Sanders found small pieces of bark and a few dried leaves. Sanders speculated whether the man had caught his final chill while gathering these once-crystallized objects from the forest.

Suzanne Clair did not appear at breakfast. When Sanders arrived at the Clairs' bungalow and was shown into the dining-room by the houseboy, Max Clair greeted him with a raised forefinger.

"Suzanne is sleeping," he told Sanders. "She had quite a night, poor dear—a lot of natives are hanging around in the bush, hoping to reap themselves a harvest of diamonds, I suppose. They've brought their sick with them, incurables for the most part. What about you, Edward? How do you feel this morning?"

"Well enough," Sanders said. "Thanks for the suit, by the way."

"Your own is dry now," Max said. "One of the boys pressed it earlier this morning. If you want to change—?"

"That's all right. This one is warmer, anyway." Sanders felt the blue serge fabric. The darker material in some way seemed more appropriate to his present meeting with Suzanne than his cotton tropical suit, a fitting disguise for this nether world where she slept by day and appeared only at night.

Max ate his breakfast with relish, working with both hands at his grapefruit. Since their meeting the previous night he had relaxed completely, almost as if Suzanne's absence gave him his first chance to lower his guard with Sanders. At the same time, Sanders guessed that he had been deliberately allowed his few minutes alone with Suzanne, to make his own brief judgment, if any, on why she and Max had come to Mont Royal.

"Edward, you haven't told me yet about your visit to the site yesterday. What exactly happened?"

Sanders glanced across the table, puzzled by Max's air of detachment. "You've probably seen as much as I have—the whole forest is vitrifying. By the way, do you know Thorensen at all?"

"Our telephone line goes through his mine office. I've met him a few times—that suit belonged to one of his engineers. He's always up to some private game of his own."

"What about this woman living with him—Serena Ventress? I take it their affair is common gossip here?"

"Not at all—Ventress, you say her name is? Probably some cocotte he picked up in a Libreville dance-hall."

"Not exactly." Sanders decided to say no more. As they finished breakfast he described his arrival at Port Matarre and the journey to Mont Royal, concluding with his visit to the inspection site. At the end, as they walked out past the empty wards on either side of the courtyard, he hinted at Professor Tatlin's explanation of the Hubble Effect and what he himself felt to be its real significance.

Max, however, seemed to have little interest in all this. Obviously he regarded the crystallizing forest as a freak of nature that would soon exhaust itself and let him get on with the job of nursing Suzanne. Sanders's oblique references to her he sidestepped deftly. With some pride he showed Sanders around the hospital, pointing out the additional wards and X-ray facilities which he and Suzanne had introduced during their short stay.

"Believe me, Edward, it's been quite a job, though I wouldn't take too much credit for ourselves. The mine companies provide most of the patients and consequently most of the money."

They were walking along the perimeter fence on the eastern side of the hospital. In the distance, beyond the single-story buildings, they could see the full extent of the forest, its soft light shining like a stained-glass canopy in the morning sun. Although still held back by the perimeter road near the Bourbon Hotel, the affected zone seemed to have spread several miles down-river, extending itself through the forested areas along the banks. Two hundred feet above the jungle the air seemed to glitter continuously, as if the crystallizing atoms were deliquescing in the wind and being replaced by those rising from the forest below.

The sounds of shouting and the thwacks of bamboo canes distracted Sanders. Fifty yards away a group of hospital porters were moving through the trees on the other side of the fence. They were driving back a throng of natives that Sanders noticed sitting in the shadows under the branches. In what seemed to be a show of strength, the porters blew their whistles and beat the ground around the natives' feet.

Looking beneath the trees, Sanders realized that there were at least two hundred of the natives, hunched together in small groups around their bundles and sticks, gazing out at the distant forest with dead eyes. All of them appeared to be crippled or diseased, with deformed faces and skeleton-like shoulders and arms. Those driven back retreated a few yards into the trees, dragging their sick with them, but the others sat their ground. They seemed unaware of the sticks and whistles. Sanders guessed that they were not drawn to the hospital by any hopes of help and attention, but regarded it merely as a temporary shield between the forest and themselves.

"Max, who the devil—?" Sanders stepped over the wire fence. The nearest group was twenty yards from him, the dark bodies almost invisible in the refuse and undergrowth below the trees.

"Some mendicant tribe," Max explained, following

Sanders over the fence. He acknowledged the salute of one of the porters. "Don't worry about them, they move around here all the time. Believe me, they don't really want help."

"But, Max—" Sanders walked a few paces across the clearing. The natives had so far watched him without expression, but now, as he approached them, they at last showed some reaction. An old man with a puffy head crouched down as if to shrink from Sanders's gaze. Another with mutilated hands hid them between his knees. There seemed to be no children, but here and there Sanders saw a small bundle strapped to the back of a crippled woman. Everywhere there was the same stirring movement as they shifted slowly in their places, little more than their shoulders moving as if aware that there was no possibility of hiding themselves.

"Max, these are—"

Clair took his arm. He started to pull Sanders back to the fence. "Yes, Edward, they are. They're lepers. They follow you across the world, don't they? I'm sorry we can't do anything for them."

"But Max—!" Sanders swung round. He pointed to the deserted wards within the compound. "The hospital's empty! Why have you turned them out?"

"We haven't." Clair looked away from the trees. "They come from a small camp—hardly a *léproserie*—which one of the Catholic fathers kept going. When he left they just drifted off into the bush. It was badly run, anyway, all he did for them was say a few prayers, and not many of those, if what I've heard is true. Now they've come back—it's the light from the forest, I suppose—"

"But why not take some of them in? You've got enough room for a few dozen cases."

"Edward, we're not equipped to deal with them. Even if we wanted to, it wouldn't work. Believe me, I've got to think of Suzanne. We all have our difficulties, you know."

"Of course." Sanders collected himself. "I understand, Max. You've both done more than your share."

Max climbed the fence into the compound. The porters had moved along the trees and were now driving back the last of the lepers, rapping the older ones and cripples over their legs when they were slow to move.

"I'll be in my surgery, Edward. Perhaps we can have a drink at eleven. Let one of the porters know if you go out."

Sanders waved to him, then walked away along the clearing. The porters had completed their job and were going back to the gatehouse, canes over their shoulders. The lepers had retreated into the deep shadows, almost out of sight, but Sanders could feel their eyes staring through him at the forest beyond, the one link between this barely recognizable residue of humanity and the world around it.

"Doctor! Dr. Sanders!"

Sanders turned to see Louise Peret coming toward him from an army staff car parked by the entrance. She waved to the French lieutenant watching from the driving window. He saluted her with a flourish and drove off.

"Louise—Aragon said you were coming this morning."

Louise reached him. Smiling broadly, she took his arm.

"I almost didn't recognize you, Edward. This suit, it's like a disguise."

"I feel I need it now." With a half-laugh Sanders pointed to the trees twenty yards from them, but Louise failed to notice the lepers sitting in the shadows.

"Aragon told me you'd been caught in the forest," she went on, glancing critically at Sanders. "But you seem all in one piece. I've been talking to Dr. Tatlin, the physicist, he's explained all his theories about the forest —very complicated, believe me, all about the stars and time, you'll be amazed when I tell you."

"I'm sure I will." Happy to listen to her blithe chatter, Sanders slipped his arm through hers and steered her along the clearing toward the group of chalets at the rear of the hospital. After the antiseptic odors and the atmosphere of illness and compromise with life, Louise's brisk stride and fresh body seemed to come from a forgotten world. Her white skirt and blouse shone against the dust and the somber trees with their hidden audience. Feeling her hips against his own, Sanders almost believed for a moment that he was walking away with her for ever from Mont Royal, the hospital and the forest.

"Louise!" With a laugh he broke into her rapid résumé of her evening at the army base. "For God's sake, shut up. You may not realize it, but you're giving me a catalogue of all the exchange officers at the camp!"

"I'm not! What do you mean? Hey, where are you taking me?"

"Coffee—for you. A drink for me. We'll go to my chalet, Max's houseboy will bring some over for us."

Louise hesitated. "All right. But what about—?"

"Suzanne?" Sanders shrugged. "She's asleep."

"What? Now?"

"She always sleeps during the day—at night she has to run the dispensary. To tell the truth, I've hardly seen her." He added hastily, aware that this was not necessarily the answer Louise wanted to hear: "It was pointless coming here—the whole thing has been a complete anti-climax."

Louise nodded at this. "Good," she said, as if only half-convinced. "Perhaps that's as it should be. And your friend—the husband?"

Before Sanders could reply Louise had stopped and taken his arm. Startled, she pointed under the trees. Here, away from the road and the gatehouse, the lepers had been driven back only a few yards, and their watching faces were plainly visible. "Edward! There, those people! What are they?"

"They're human," Sanders said evenly. With faint sarcasm he added: "Don't be frightened."

"I'm not. But what are they doing? My God, there are hundreds of them! They were here all the time we were talking."

"I don't suppose they bothered to listen." Sanders motioned Louise through a gap in the fence. "Poor devils, they're just sitting there spellbound."

"How do you mean? By me?"

Sanders laughed aloud at this. Taking Louise's arm again, he held it tightly. "My dear, what have those Frenchmen been doing to you? *I'm* spellbound by you, but I'm afraid those people are only interested in the forest."

They walked across the small courtyard and entered

Sanders's chalet. He rang the bell for the Clairs' house-boy and then ordered some coffee for Louise and whisky and soda for himself. When these arrived they settled themselves in the lounge. Sanders switched on the over-head fan and removed his jacket.

"Taking off your disguise now?" Louise asked.

"You're right." Sanders pulled up the footstool and sat down in front of the settee. "I'm glad you're here, Louise. You make the place seem less like an unmade grave."

He reached forward and took the coffee cup and saucer from her hands. He rose to sit down beside her and then walked over to the window which looked out on to the Clairs' bungalow. He lowered the plastic blind.

"Edward, for a man so uncertain of his real nature you can be very calculating." Louise watched him with amusement as he sat down on the settee beside her. Pretending to hold off his arm, she asked: "Are you still testing yourself, my dear? A woman likes to know her proper role at all times, this one most of all." When Sanders said nothing she pointed to the blind. "I thought you said she was asleep. Or do the vampires here fly by day?"

As she laughed Sanders put his hand firmly on her chin. "Day and night—do they mean much any longer?"

They ate lunch together in the chalet. Afterwards, Sanders described his experiences in the forest.

"I remember, Louise, when I first arrived in Port Matarre you told me it was the day of the spring equinox. Of course, it hadn't occurred to me before, but I realize now just how far everything in the world outside the forest was being divided into light and dark —you could see it perfectly in Port Matarre, that strange light in the arcades and in the jungle around the town, and even in the people there, dark and light twins of each other. Looking back, they all seem to pair off—Ventress with his white suit and the mine-owner Thorensen with his black gang. They're fighting each other now over this dying woman somewhere in the forest. Then there are Suzanne and yourself—you haven't met her but she's your exact opposite, very elusive and shadowy. When *you* arrived this morning, Louise, it was as if you'd stepped out of the sun. Again, there's Balthus, that priest, with his death-mask face, though God alone knows who his twin is."

"Perhaps you, Edward."

"You may be right—I suppose he's trying to free himself from what's left of his faith, just as I'm trying to escape from Fort Isabelle and the *léproserie*—Radek pointed that out to me, poor fellow."

"But this division, Edward, into black and white— why? They're what you care to make them."

"Are they? I suspect it goes deeper than that. There may well be some fundamental distinction between light and dark that we inherit from the earliest living creatures. After all, the response to light is a response to all the possibilities of life itself. For all we know, this division is the strongest one there is—perhaps even the *only* one—reinforced everyday for hundreds of millions of years. In its simplest sense time keeps this going, and now that time is withdrawing we're beginning to see the contrasts in everything more clearly. It's not a matter of identifying any moral notions with light and dark—I don't take sides between Ventress and Thorensen. Isolated now they're both grotesques, but perhaps the forest will bring them together. There, in that place of rainbows, nothing is distinguished from anything else."

"And Suzanne—your dark lady—what does she mean for you, Edward?"

"I'm not sure—obviously she stands in some way for the *léproserie* and whatever *that* means—the dark side of the equinox. Believe me, I recognize now that my motives for working at the *léproserie* weren't altogether humanitarian, but merely accepting that doesn't help me. Of course there's a dark side of the psyche, and I suppose all one can do is find the other face and try to reconcile the two—it's happening out there in the forest."

"How long are you staying?" Louise asked. "In Mont Royal?"

"Another few days. I can't leave straightaway. From my point of view coming here has been a complete failure, but I've hardly seen either of them and they may need my help."

"Edward—" Louise walked over to the window. Pulling on the blind, she raised the blades so that they let in the afternoon light. Silhouetted against the sun, her white suit and pale skin became suddenly dark. As she played with the string, opening and closing the blind, her slim figure was lit and then eclipsed like an image in a solar shutter. "Edward, there's an army launch going back to Port Matarre tomorrow. In the afternoon. I've decided to go."

"But, Louise—"

"I must go." She faced him, her chin raised. "There's no hope of finding Anderson—he must be dead by now—and I owe it to the bureau to get my story out."

"Story? My dear, you're thinking in terms of trivialities." Sanders went over to the whisky decanter on the bare sideboard. "Louise, I'd hoped you could stay on with me—" He broke off, aware that Louise was putting him to the test and not wanting to upset her. Whatever his references to Suzanne, he knew that he would have to stay with her and Max for the time being. If anything, Suzanne's leprosy had increased his need to remain with her. Despite her aloofness the previous night, Sanders knew that he was the only person to understand the real nature of her affliction and its meaning for them both.

To Louise, as she picked up her handbag, he said: "I'll ask Max to call the base and send a car for you."

During the rest of the afternoon Sanders remained in the chalet, watching the corona of light that lay over the distant forest. Behind him, beyond the perimeter fence, the lepers had moved forward again through the trees. As the afternoon light faded, the brilliance of the sun was still held within the crystal forest, and the old men and women came to the edge of the trees and waited there like nervous wraiths.

After dusk Suzanne appeared again. Whether she had really been asleep or, like Sanders, sitting in her room behind drawn blinds, he had no means of knowing, but at dinner she seemed even more withdrawn than at their previous meeting, eating with a kind of compulsive nervousness as if forcing down food that lacked all flavor. She had finished each of the courses when Sanders and Max were still talking over their wine. The black velvet curtain behind her—obviously placed against this single window for Sanders's benefit—made her dark robe almost invisible in the dim light, and from the far end of the table, where she had placed Sanders, even the white powdered mask of her face seemed a veiled blur.

"Did Max take you on a tour of our hospital?" she asked. "I hope you were impressed?"

"Very," Sanders said. "It has no patients." He added: "I'm surprised you need to spend any time at all in the dispensary."

"Quite a number of the natives come along during the night," Max explained. "During the daytime they're hanging around near the forest. One of the drivers told me that they're starting to take their sick and dying into the affected area. A kind of instant mummification, I suppose."

"But far more splendid," Suzanne said. "Like a fly in the amber of its own tears or a fossil millions of years old, making a diamond of its body for us. I hope the army let them through."

"They can't stop them," Max rejoined. "If these people want to commit suicide it's their affair. The army is too busy anyway evacuating themselves." He turned to Sanders. "It's almost comical, Edward. As soon as they put the camp down somewhere they have to uproot the whole thing and back off another quarter of a mile."

"How fast is the area spreading?"

"About a hundred feet a day, or more. According to the army radio network things are getting to the panic stage in the focal area in Florida. Half the state has been evacuated, already the zone there extends from the Everglades swamps all the way to Miami."

Suzanne raised her glass at this. "Can you imagine that, Edward? An entire city! All those hundreds of white hotels transformed into stained glass—it must be like Venice in the days of Titian and Veronese, or Rome with dozens of St. Peters."

Max laughed. "Suzanne, you make it sound like the new Jerusalem. Before you could turn around I'm afraid you'd find yourself an angel in a rose window."

After dinner, Sanders waited for Clair to leave and give him a few moments alone with Suzanne, but Max took a chess set from the blackwood cabinet and set up the pieces. As he and Sanders played the opening moves Suzanne excused herself and slipped out.

Sanders waited an hour for her to come back. At ten o'clock he resigned his game and said good night to Max, leaving him mulling over the possibilities of the end game.

Unable to sleep, Sanders wandered around his chalet, drinking what was left of the whisky in the decanter. In one of the empty rooms he found a stack of French illustrated magazines and leafed through the pages, scanning the by-lines of the articles for Louise's name.

On an impulse he left the chalet and went out into the

darkness. He walked toward the perimeter fence. Twenty yards from the wire he could see the lepers sitting under the trees in the moonlight. They had come forward on to the open ground, exposing themselves to the moonlight like bathers under a midnight sun. One or two were shuffling about through the lines of people half-asleep on the ground or squatting on their bundles.

Hiding himself in the shadows behind the chalet, Sanders turned and followed their gaze. The vast outspill of light rose from the forest, its extent broken only by the dim white form of the Bourbon Hotel.

Sanders walked back into the compound. Crossing the courtyard, he made his way to the perimeter fence as it turned in the direction of the ruined hotel, which was now hidden by the intervening trees. A path led toward it through the trees, passing the abandoned mine-works. Sanders stepped over the fence, then walked through the dark air toward the hotel.

Ten minutes later, as he stood at the top of the wide steps that led down among the tumbled columns, he saw Suzanne Clair walking in the moonlight below him. In a few places the affected zone had crossed the highway, and small patches of the scrub along the roadside had begun to vitrify. Their drab leaves gave off a faint luminescence. Suzanne walked among them, her long robe sweeping across the brittle ground. Sanders could see that her shoes and the train of her robe were beginning to crystallize, the minute prisms glancing in the moonlight.

Sanders made his way down the steps, his feet cutting at the shards of marble between the columns. Turning, Suzanne saw him approach. For a moment she flinched toward the road, then recognized him and hurried up the weed-grown drive.

"Edward—!"

Sanders reached out to take her hands, afraid that she might stumble, but Suzanne slipped past and pressed herself to his chest. Sanders embraced her, feeling her dark hair against his cheek. Her waist and shoulders were like ice, the silk robe chilling his hands.

"Suzanne, I thought you might be here." He tried to move her away, so that he could see her face, but she still held on to him with the strong grip of a dancer moving with her partner through an intricate step. Her eyes were turned away so that she seemed to speak from the ruins beyond his left shoulder.

"Edward, I come here every night." She pointed to the upper stories of the white hotel. "I was there yesterday, I watched you come out of the forest! Do you know, Edward, your clothes were glowing!"

Sanders nodded, then walked with her up the drive to the steps. As if straightening her hair, Suzanne held one hand to her forehead between them, the other clasping his own hand to her cold waist.

"Does Max know you're here?" Sanders asked. "He may send one of the houseboys to keep an eye on you."

"My dear Edward!" Suzanne laughed for the first time. "Max has no idea, he's asleep, poor man—he realizes he's living on the edges of a nightmare—" She stopped, checking herself in case Sanders might guess that this referred to her own condition. "The forest, that is. He's never understood what it means. You do, Edward, I could see that straightaway."

"Perhaps—" They climbed the steps past the drums of the toppled columns and entered the great hall. High above, the cupola over the staircase had fallen through and Sanders could see a cluster of stars, but the light from the forest below cast the hall into almost complete darkness. Immediately he felt Suzanne relax. Taking his hand, she guided him past the shattered chandelier at the foot of the staircase.

They walked up to the second floor, and then turned into a corridor on their left. Through the broken panels Sanders saw the worm-eaten hulks of tall wardrobes and collapsed bedposts, like the derelict monuments in some mausoleum to the hotel's forgotten past.

"Here we are." Suzanne stepped through a locked door whose central panels had fallen in. In the room beyond, the empire furniture was in place, a desk stood in the corner by the window, and a mirrorless dressing table framed the forest below. Dust and wormwood lay on the floor, small footprints winding through them.

Suzanne sat down on one side of the bed, opening her robe with the placid gestures of a wife returning home with her husband. "What do you think of it, Edward, —my pied à terre, or is it nearer the clouds than that?"

Sanders glanced around the dusty room, looking for some personal trace of Suzanne. Apart from the footprints on the floor there was nothing of her there, as if she dwelled like a ghost among the empty chambers of the white hotel.

"I like the room," he said. "It has a magnificent view of the forest."

"I only come here in the evening, and then the dust looks like moonlight."

Sanders sat down on the bed beside her. He glanced up at the ceiling, half-afraid that at any moment the hotel might crumble and collapse into a dust-filled pit, carrying Suzanne and himself down into its maw. He waited for the darkness to clear, aware of the contrast between Suzanne and this room in the derelict hotel with its moonlit empire furniture and the functional but sun-filled chalet where he and Louise had made love that morning. Louise's body had lain beside him like a piece of the sun, a golden odalisque trapped for Pharaoh in his tomb. As now, in turn, he held Suzanne's cold body in his arms, his hands avoiding her face, which lay beside him in the darkness, its pale lantern like a closing moon, he remembered Ventress's "We're running out of time, Sanders—" As time withdrew, his relationship with Suzanne, drained of everything but the image of leprosy and whatever this stood for in his mind, had begun to dissolve into the dust that surrounded them wherever they moved outside the forest.

"Suzanne—" He sat up beside her, trying to massage some warmth into his hands. Her breasts had been like goblets of ice. "Tomorrow I'm going back to Port Matarre. It's time for me to leave."

"What?" Suzanne drew the robe across herself, sealing the white outline of her body into the darkness. "But, Edward, I thought you'd—"

Sanders took her hand. "My dear, apart from everything I owe Max there are my patients at Isabelle. I can't just leave them."

"They were my patients as well. The forest is spreading everywhere, there's no more you or I can do for them."

"Perhaps not—I may only be thinking of myself again —and you, Suzanne—"

While he spoke she had left the bed and now stood in front of him, the dark robe brushing the dust from the floor. "Stay with us for a week, Edward. Derain won't mind, he knew you were coming here. In a week—"

"In a week we may all have to go. Believe me, Suzanne, I've been trapped in the forest."

She walked toward him, her face raised in a shaft of moonlight as if about to kiss him on the mouth. Then he realized that this was far from being a romantic gesture. At last Suzanne was showing him her face.

"Edward, just now, do you know to whom you—made love to?"

Sanders touched her shoulder with one hand, trying to reassure her. "Suzanne, I do know. Last night—"

"What?" She turned away from him, hiding her face again. "What do you mean?"

Sanders followed her across the room. "I'm sorry, Suzanne. It may sound hollow comfort, but I carry those lesions as much as you do."

Before he could reach her she had slipped through the door. He picked up his jacket and saw her moving swiftly down the long corridor to the staircase. When he reached the entrance hall she was more than fifty yards ahead of him, running through the tumbled columns, her dark gown like an immense veil as she moved along the crystalline pathways away from the white hotel.

Duel
with a
crocodile

At midnight, as he lay half-asleep in his room at the rear of the chalet, Dr. Sanders heard the sounds of a distant commotion from the compound of the hospital. Almost too tired to sleep, and yet sufficiently exhausted not to listen more closely, he ignored the raised voices and the flickering beam of the Land-Rover's searchlight carried over the roof and reflected off the tall trees outside.

Later, the noise began again. The engine of an antiquated truck was being hand-started in the compound. As it coughed and sneezed and the voices chattered around it, he heard more footsteps running in and out of the chalets. All the servants seemed to be up, wandering in and out of the rooms across the courtyard and slamming the cupboard doors.

When he saw someone with a torch inspecting the vegetation outside his window Sanders climbed from his bed and dressed.

In the dining-room of the chalet he found one of the houseboys looking through the open window into the forest.

"What's going on?" Dr. Sanders asked. "What the devil are you doing in here? Where's Dr. Clair?"

The houseboy pointed toward the compound. "Dr. Clair with truck, sir. Trouble in forest, he go to look."

"What sort of trouble?" Sanders walked over to the window. "Is the forest moving nearer?"

"No, sir, not moving. Dr. Clair say you sleep, sir."

"Where's Mrs. Clair? Is she around?"

"No, sir. Mrs. Clair busy now."

"What do you mean?" Dr. Sanders pressed. "I thought she was on night duty. Come on, man, what is it?"

The houseboy hesitated, his lips soundlessly forming the polite formulas which Max had left him for Sanders's benefit. He was about to blurt something out when the sound of footsteps crossed the courtyard. Sanders went to the door as Max Clair came toward him, followed by two porters.

"Max! What's going on—are you starting to evacuate?"

Clair stopped in front of him. His mouth was clenched, his chin lowered so that the sweat on his domed head shone in the torch-light. "Edward—have you got Suzanne in there with you?"

"What?" Sanders stepped back from the door, beckoning Clair inside. "My dear fellow— She's gone! Where?"

"I wish we knew." Clair walked up to the door. He glanced inside the chalet, uncertain whether to take advantage of Sanders's gesture. "She went off a couple of hours ago, God only knows where—you haven't seen her?"

"Not since earlier this evening." Sanders began to button the sleeves of his shirt. "Come on, Max, let's go after her!"

Clair held up his hand. "Not you, Edward. I have

enough problems, believe me. There are one or two settlements up in the hills," he said, unconvincingly. "She may have gone to visit the sick-bays. You stay here and keep things together—I'll take the Land-Rover and a couple of men. The others can go in the truck and keep an eye on the Bourbon Hotel."

Sanders began to argue with him, but Clair turned and strode off. Sanders followed him into the drive and watched him climb into the car.

Sanders turned to the houseboy. "So she's gone back into the forest—poor woman!"

The houseboy glanced at him. "You know, sir?"

"No, but I'm certain all the same. Each of us has something we can't bear to be reminded of. Tell the driver of the truck to wait, he can give me a lift down to the hotel."

The houseboy held his arm. "You going, sir—to the forest?"

"Of course. She's there somewhere—that's a judgment on myself I have to acknowledge."

The antiquated engine of the truck had come to life, its din throbbing all over the hospital. As Sanders climbed over the tailboard it started off and made a slow circuit of the fountain. Half a dozen of the native orderlies sat up behind the driver.

They reached the main highway five minutes later, then rumbled on through the darkness towards the white hulk of the Bourbon Hotel. The truck stopped in the weed-grown drive, its searchlight playing on the forest. As it swept across the crystalline trees, like an immense tipping of broken glass, the white prisms glittered as far away as the river half a mile to the south.

Jumping down from the tailboard, Dr. Sanders went over to the driver. None of the men had seen Suzanne leave, but from their careful watch over the forest they obviously all assumed that she had entered it. However, from the confused mêlée around the vehicle it was equally plain that they had no intention of following Suzanne. When Sanders pressed the driver he made some muttered reference to the "white phantoms" that patrolled its inner reaches—glimpses, perhaps of Ventress and Thorensen in pursuit of each other, or of Radek stumbling toward his lost grave.

Five minutes later, when he saw that the search party was no closer to forming itself—the driver insisted on remaining by his searchlight, and the other men had moved off to the Bourbon Hotel and squatted down with their cheroots among the fallen columns—Dr. Sanders set off alone along the highway. To his left, the glitter of the forest threw the cold moonlight across the macadam at his feet, and lit up the entrance to a small side-road that ran toward the river. Sanders looked down this narrow defile that led away into the illuminated world. For a moment he hesitated, listening to the fading voices of the natives. Then he pressed his hands into his pockets and moved along the verges of the road, picking his way among the glass spurs that rose more and more thickly around him.

In fifteen minutes he reached the river, and crossed a ruined bridge that tilted down on to the frozen surface like a jeweled web, its girders hung with silver. The white surface of the river wound away around the frosted trees. The few craft along the banks were now so heavily encrusted that they were barely recognizable. Their light seemed darker and more intense, as if they were sealing their brilliance within themselves.

By this time his suit had begun to glow again in the dark, the fine frost forming crystal spurs on the fabric. Everywhere the process of crystallization was more advanced, and his shoes were enclosed within bowls of prisms.

Mont Royal was empty. Limping in and out of the deserted streets, the white buildings looming around him like sepulchers, he reached the harbor. Standing on the jetty, he could see across the frozen surface of the river to the cataract in the distance. Even higher now, it formed an impenetrable barrier between himself and the lost army somewhere to the south.

Shortly before dawn he walked back through the town, in the hope of finding the summer house where Thorensen and his dying bride were sheltering. He passed a small patch of pavement that remained clear of all growth, below the broken window of one of the mine depositories. Handfuls of looted stones were scattered across the pavement, ruby and emerald rings, topaz brooches and pendants, intermingled with countless smaller stones and industrial diamonds. This abandoned harvest glittered coldly in the moonlight.

As he stood among the stones Sanders noticed that the crystal outgrowths from his shoes were dissolving, melting like icicles exposed to sudden heat. Pieces of the crust fell away and deliquesced, vanishing into the air.

Then he realized why Thorensen had brought the jewels to the young woman, and why she had seized on them so eagerly. By some optical or electromagnetic freak, the intense focus of light within the stones simultaneously produced a compression of time, so that the discharge of light from the surfaces reversed the process of crystallization. Perhaps it was this gift of time which accounted for the eternal appeal of precious gems, as well as of all baroque painting and architecture. Their intricate crests and cartouches, occupying more than their own volume of space, so seemed to contain a greater ambient time, providing that unmistakable premonition of immortality sensed within St. Peter's or the palace at Nymphenburg. By contrast, the architecture of the twentieth century, characteristically one of rectangular unornamented façades, of simple Euclidean space and time, was that of the New World, confident of its firm footing in the future and indifferent to those pangs of mortality which haunted the mind of old Europe.

Dr. Sanders knelt down and filled his pockets with the stones, cramming them into his shirt and cuffs. He sat back against the front of the depository, the semi-circle of smooth pavement like a miniature patio, at whose edges the crystal undergrowth glittered with the intensity of a spectral garden. Pressed to his cold skin, the hard faces of the jewels seemed to warm him, and within a few seconds he fell into an exhausted sleep.

He woke into brilliant sunshine in a street of temples, where rainbows spangled the gilded air with a blaze of colors. Shielding his eyes, he lay back and looked up at the roof-tops, their gold tiles inlaid with row upon row of colored gems, like pavilions in the temple quarter of Bangkok.

A hand pulled at his shoulder. Trying to sit up, Sanders found that the semi-circle of clear pavement had vanished, and his body lay sprawled in a bed of sprouting needles. The growth had been most rapid in the entrance to the depository, and his right arm was encased in a mass of crystalline spurs, three or four inches long, that reached almost to his shoulder. Inside this frozen gauntlet, almost too heavy to lift, his fingers were outlined in a maze of rainbows.

Sanders dragged himself to his knees, tearing away some of the crystals. He found the bearded man in the white suit crouching behind him, his shotgun in his hands.

"Ventress!" With a cry, Sanders raised his jeweled arm. In the sunlight the faint nodes of the gem-stones he had stuffed into his cuff shone in the effloresced tissues of his arm like inlaid stars. "Ventress, for God's sake!"

His shout distracted Ventress from his scrutiny of the light-filled street. His small face with its bright eyes was transfigured by strange colors that mottled his skin and drew out the pale blues and violets of his beard. His suit radiated a thousand bands of color.

He knelt down beside Sanders, trying to replace the strip of crystals torn from his arm. Before he could speak there was a roar of gunfire and the glass trellis encrusted to the doorway shattered in a shower of fragments. Ventress flinched behind Sanders, then pulled himself through the window. As another shot was fired down the street they ran past the looted counters into a strong room where the door of a safe stood open on to a jumble of metal cash boxes. Ventress snapped back the lids on the empty trays, and then began to scoop together the few small jewels scattered across the floor.

Stuffing them into Sanders's empty pockets, he pulled him through a window into the rear alley, and from there into the adjacent street, transformed by the overhead lattices into a tunnel of vermilion light. They stopped at the first turning, and Ventress beckoned to the forest fifty yards away.

"Run, run! Anywhere, through the forest! It's all you can do!"

He pushed Sanders forward with the butt of his shotgun, whose breech was now encrusted by a mass of silver crystals, like a medieval flintlock. Sanders raised his arm. The jeweled spurs danced in the sunlight like a swarm of fireflies. "My arm, Ventress! It's reached my shoulder!"

"Run! Nothing else can help you!" Ventress's illuminated face flickered with anger, almost as if he were impatient of Sanders's refusal to accept the forest. "Don't waste the stones, they won't last you forever!"

Forcing himself to run, Sanders set off toward the forest, where he entered the first of the caves of light. He whirled his arm like a clumsy propeller, and felt the crystals recede slightly. With luck he soon reached a small tributary of the river that wound in from the harbor, and hurled himself like a wild man along its petrified surface.

For hours he raced through the forest, all sense of time lost to him. If he stopped for more than a minute the crystal bands would seize his neck and shoulder, and he forced himself on, only pausing to slump exhausted on the glass beaches. Then, he pressed the jewels to his face, warding off the glacé sheath. But their power faded, and as the facets blunted they turned into nodes of unpolished silica. Meanwhile, those embedded within the crystal tissues of his arm shone with undiminished brilliance.

At last, as he ran through the trees at the edge of the river, his arm whirling before him, he saw the gilt spire of the summer house. Stumbling across the fused sand, he made his way toward it. By now the vitrification of the forest had sealed the small pavilion into the surrounding trees, and only the steps and the doorway above remained clear, but for Sanders it still held a faint hope of sanctuary. The casements and jointing of the balcony were ornamented with the heraldic devices of some bizarre baroque architecture.

Sanders stopped a few yards from the steps and looked up at the sealed door. He turned and gazed back across the widening channel of the river. Its jeweled surface glowed in the sunlight, marbled like the pink crust of a salt lake. Two hundred yards away Thorensen's motor-cruiser still sat in its pool of clear water at the confluence of the subterranean streams.

As he watched, two men moved about on the foredeck of the cruiser. They were partly hidden by the starting cannon in front of the mast, but one of them, bands of surgical tape dividing his naked body into black and white halves, Sanders recognized as Kagwa, Thorensen's assistant.

Sanders walked a few steps toward the cruiser, debating whether to reach the edge of the petrified surface and swim across the pool. Although the crystals might begin to dissolve in the water, he feared that the weight of his arm would first sink him to the bottom.

There was a flash of light from the muzzle of the cannon. A moment later, as the ground shifted slightly, Sanders caught a glimpse of a three-inch ball crossing the air toward him. With a sharp whistle it passed over his head and crashed into the petrified trees twenty yards from the summer house. Then the loud boom of the explosion reached him from the cruiser. Reflected off the hard surface of the river, the echoes rolled around the walls of the forest, drumming at Sanders's head.

Uncertain which way to move, he ran toward a patch of undergrowth near the steps of the summer house. Kneeling down, he tried to conceal his arm among the crystalline fronds. The two natives on board the cruiser were reloading the cannon, the big mulatto down on one knee as he worked the ramrod in and out of the barrel.

"Sanders—!" The low voice, little more than a harsh whisper, came from a few yards on Sanders's left. He looked around, peering up at the sealed door of the summer house. Then, below the steps, a hand reached out and waved at him.

"Here! Under the house!"

Sanders ran over to the steps. In the narrow hollow below the platform of the summer house, Ventress was crouching behind one of the stilts, shotgun in hand.

"Get down! Before they take another shot at you!" As Sanders slid backwards through the small interval

Ventress seized one shoe and hauled him in, twisting his foot with an irritable flourish.

"Lie *down!* By God, Sanders, you take your chances!"

His mottled face pressed toward Sanders as he lay against the side of the hollow. Then Ventress looked out again at the river and the distant cruiser. His flintlock lay in front of him, its ornamented barrel following every movement as the light outside varied its patterns.

Sanders gazed around the hollow, wondering if Thorensen had taken Serena with him and abandoned the summer house, hoping to trap Ventress there, or whether the latter had reached the pavilion first after the attack that morning in the streets of Mont Royal.

The wooden boards over their heads had vitrified into a rock-like glass, but the outlines of a trapdoor could still be seen in the center. On the ground below, a steel bayonet lay among a few shards laboriously chipped from the edges of the trapdoor.

Ventress pointed curtly to the trapdoor. "You can have a go in a moment. It's damned hard work."

Sanders sat forward. Lifting his arm, he turned over so that he could see across the river.

"Serena—your wife—is she still here?"

Ventress looked up at the beams over their heads. "I'll be with her soon. It's been a long search." Checking himself, he peered along his barrel, examining the sprays of frozen grass that skirted the banks before he spoke again. "So you saw her, Sanders?"

"Only for a minute. I told Thorensen to get her out of here."

Leaving his gun, Ventress scrambled across to

Sanders. Kneeling in the hollow like a luminous mole, he peered into Sanders's eyes. "Sanders, tell me—I haven't seen her yet! My God!" He drummed on the wooden beams, sending a dead echo through the platform.

"She's—all right," Sanders said. "Most of the time she's asleep. How did you get here?"

His mind elsewhere, Ventress stared at him. Then he crawled back to his shotgun. He beckoned Sanders forward. He pointed to the bank fifty feet away. Lying face upwards among the grass, the spurs of frost from his crystallizing body merging him into the undergrowth, was one of Thorensen's men.

"Poor Thorensen," Ventress murmured. "One by one they're leaving him. He'll be alone soon, Sanders."

There was another flash from the cannon on board the cruiser. The craft backed slightly in the water, and the steel ball arched through the air, striking the trees a hundred yards from the summer house. As the boom of the explosion drummed around the river, shaking the rails of the balcony, Sanders noticed the light driven from his arm in a series of soft pulses. The surface of the river shifted and settled itself, blades of carmine light lancing into the air.

Kagwa and the mulatto knelt down by the cannon again and began to reload it. Sanders said: "Bad shooting. But Serena—if she's here why are they trying to hit the summer house?"

"They're not, my dear fellow." Ventress was watching the undergrowth along the banks, as if taking no chances that Thorensen might not try to steal up on the summer house during the distractions of the artillery display. After a moment, apparently satisfied, he relaxed. "He has other plans for his big gun. His idea is to loosen the river with the noise—then he can bring his boat right up to the summer house and blast me out of here."

Sure enough, during the next hour a series of dull explosions punctuated the still air. The two Negroes worked away at the cannon, and at intervals of five minutes or so there was a brief flash and one of the steel balls flew across the river. As they rebounded off the bank and trees the echoes of the reports struck vivid red lanes through the petrified surface.

Each time Sanders's jeweled arm and Ventress's suit shed rainbows of light around them.

"What are you doing here, Sanders?" Ventress asked during one of the lulls. There were no signs of Thorensen, and Kagwa and the mulatto worked without supervision. Ventress had crawled back to the trapdoor and was chipping away with the bayonet, now and then pausing to press his head to the platform and listen for any sounds above. "I thought you'd got out?"

"The wife of a colleague of mine at Isabelle—Suzanne Clair—ran off into the forest last night. It was partly my fault." Sanders looked down at the crystal sheath on his arm. No longer having to carry its great weight around he found that he was less frightened of its monstrous appearance. Although the crystalline tissues were as cold as ice, and no movement of his hand or fingers was possible, the nerves and sinews seemed to have taken on a new life of their own, glowing like the hard compacted light they emitted. Only along the forearm, where he had torn away the strip of crystals, was there any marked sensation, but even here it was less one of pain than a feeling of warmth as the crystals annealed themselves.

Another explosion boomed across the river. Ventress threw the bayonet away. He scuttled back to his place near the steps.

Sanders watched the cruiser. It still remained at its mooring in the mouth of the creek, but Kagwa and the mulatto had left the cannon and gone below. Evidently the last round had been fired. Ventress pointed with a bony finger at the small trail of exhaust from the stern. The cruiser began to swing round. As it turned and the cabin windows altered their angle, they could both see a tall blond-haired man behind the wheel.

"Thorensen!" Ventress crept forward, his small body crouching with knees pressed against his chest.

Sanders picked up the bayonet in his left hand. The cruiser was moving astern, the smoke of the exhaust drifting along its hull. It stopped and straightened out.

Full ahead, the cruiser surged forward, its bows lifting through the placid water. An interval of fifty yards separated it from the nearest edge of the petrified crust. As it changed course, selecting one of the faults exposed by the bombardment, Sanders remembered Thorensen testing the lanes through the collapsing surface when Ventress had escaped from the mulatto.

Moving at twenty knots, the cruiser bore down on the edge of the pool, then drove through the thin crystals like an ice-breaker scattering surface ice out of its path. Within thirty yards its speed fell off. A few huge floes piled up across its bows, and the cruiser slewed sideways and came to a stop. There was a flurry of activity on the bridge as the men inside wrestled with the controls, and Ventress leveled his gun at the cabin windows. Three hundred feet away, the cruiser was well out of range. Around it immense faults had appeared in the surface of the river, the vivid carmine light bled off into the surrounding ice. The trees along the bank were still shaking with the impact, shedding the light from their boughs like liquid blossoms.

After a pause the cruiser backed off a few feet, then retraced its path down the lane. Fifty yards back, in the entrance to the pool, it stopped and aligned its bows.

As it drove forward again, lifting on the exposed water, Ventress reached into his jacket. From the shoulder holster he drew out the automatic pistol Sanders had smuggled through the customs.

"Take it!" Ventress leveled his shotgun at the approaching cruiser, shouting at Sanders across the breech. "Watch the bank on your side! I'll look out for Thorensen!"

This time the smooth advance of the cruiser was checked more abruptly. Hitting the heavier floes, it scattered half a dozen of the giant crystal blocks across the surface, then rammed to a half with a fifteen-degree list, its engine racing. The men on board were flung to the floor of the cabin, and it was several minutes before the cruiser righted itself and made a slow reverse passage down the channel.

The next time it approached more slowly, its bows first loosening the surface, then driving the crystal blocks out of their way.

Sanders crouched behind one of the wooden stilts, waiting for the mulatto to fire the cannon before the cruiser came within close range of Ventress. It was now only seventy-five yards from the summer house, its bridge high in the air above them. Ventress, however, seemed composed, watching the banks for any surprise attack.

The ground shook beneath the summer house as the cruiser drove again and again into the crystal pack. The smoke of its exhaust hung around them, fouling the crisp air. Each time it came a few yards closer, its bows splintering into white spars. Already the cruiser had been enveloped by a fine frost, and the mulatto knocked out the crystallizing windows of the cabin with a rifle butt. The deck rails were hung with fine spurs. Ventress maneuvered about, trying to get a shot in at the men in the cabin, but their heads were hidden behind the broken panes. Jerked up on to the surface, the blocks of damp crystals were scattered out of the cruiser's way, and the first pieces skated across to the steps of the summer house.

"Sanders!" Ventress half-stood, his face and chest exposed. "They're landlocked!"

Thirty yards away, its shattered bows rooted in a fault between two floes, the cruiser was heaving from side to side. Its engine roared and faded, then whined and fell silent. Immobile, the cruiser sat in front of them, the fine frost already transforming it into a bizarre wedding cake. Once or twice it rocked slightly as if an oar or a grappling line was being worked from a stern porthole.

Ventress kept his shotgun leveled at the cabin. Ten feet away on his right, Sanders held the automatic pistol in one hand, his other arm on the ground beside him, glowing in its own crystal life. Together they waited for Thorensen to make a move. For half an hour the cruiser was silent, the frost thickening on its decks. Spiral crests formed around the windows of the cabin and ornamented the deck rails and portholes. The shattered bows bristled like the tusks of a frozen whale. Below the bridge the cannon was transformed into a medieval firing piece, its breech embellished with exquisite horns and crests.

The afternoon light was fading. Sanders watched the bank on his right, where the vivid colors had become more somber as the sun sank behind the trees into the west.

Then, among the white sprays of grass, he saw a long silver-bodied creature shuffling along the bank. Ventress crouched beside him, peering through the dim light. They watched the jeweled snout and hooked forelegs in their crystal armor. The crocodile sidled slowly on its stomach in its ancient reptilian motion. Fully fifteen feet long, it seemed to propel itself more with its tail than by its legs. The left foreleg hung in the air frozen within the crystal armour. As it moved the light poured from the glacé eyes and from the half-opened mouth choked with jewels.

It stopped, as if sensing the two men under the summer house, and then slid forward. Five feet away, it stopped for a second time, jaws working weakly, its body crushing the grass in its path. Feeling a remote sympathy for this monster in its armor of light, unable to understand its own transfiguration, Sanders watched the blank eyes above the opening mouth.

Then, as the jeweled teeth glittered at him, Sanders realized that he was looking into a gun barrel.

Cutting off an involuntary shout, Sanders lowered his head, then moved a few feet away from the pillar. As he raised his head he saw the mouth of the crocodile open. The gun barrel came forward below the upper row of teeth, and then fired once at the shadow of the wooden pillar.

In the roar of the gun flame Sanders steadied the automatic pistol on the notched surface of his crystal arm and fired at the crocodile's head. It twisted sideways, the barrel searching for him. Inside the jeweled skin Sanders could see a man's elbows and knees on the ground. Sanders fired again at the thorax and abdomen of the carapace. With a galvanic heave the huge beast rose into the air on its hind legs and hovered there like a jeweled saurian. Then it fell over on to its side, exposing the open slit from the lower jaw to the abdomen. Strapped inside, the body of the mulatto lay face up in the dusk, his black skin illuminated by the crystal ship moored like a ghost behind him.

Feet raced along the opposite bank. With a shout Ventress rose on his knees and fired the shotgun. There was a shrill cry, and the half-bandaged figure of Kagwa fell among the sprays of grass ten yards from the summer house. He rose to his feet and stumbled past the house, no longer aware of what he was doing. For a moment the last daylight on his dark skin made him seem almost as white as the small figure of Ventress. The second shot caught him in the chest, knocking him away across the bank. He lay on his face in the edge of the shadows.

Sanders waited in the hollow as Ventress reloaded his shotgun. He scuttled about, peering at the two bodies. For a few minutes there was silence, and then he touched Sanders on the shoulder with the shotgun.

"Right, Doctor."

Sanders looked up at his expressionless face. "What do you mean?"

"It's time for you to go, Doctor. Thorensen and I are alone now."

As Sanders climbed to his feet, hesitating to expose himself, Ventress said: "Thorensen will understand. Get out of the forest, Sanders, you aren't ready to come here yet." As he spoke, Ventress's suit was covered with the jeweled scales of the crystals that had formed there.

So Sanders took his leave of Ventress. Outside, the white ship had begun to merge into the torn surface of the river. As he walked away from the summer house along the bank, leaving behind the three dead men, one still in his crocodile skin, Sanders saw nothing of Thorensen. A hundred yards from the house, where the river turned, he looked back, but Ventress was hidden below his platform. Above him the faint light of a lantern shone in the glazed windows.

At last, late that afternoon, when the deepening ruby light of dusk settled through the forest, Sanders entered a small clearing where the deep sounds of an organ reverberated among the trees. In the center was a small

church, its slim spire fused to the branches of the surrounding trees by the crystal tracery.

Raising his jeweled arm to light the oaken doors,
Sanders drove them back and entered the nave. Above
him, refracted by the stained-glass windows, a brilliant
glow of light poured down upon the altar. Listening to
the organ, Sanders leaned against the altar rail and extended his arm to the gold cross set with rubies and
emeralds. Immediately the sheath slipped and began to
dissolve, like a melting sleeve of ice. As the crystals
deliquesced the light poured from his arm like an over-
flowing fountain.

Turning his head to watch Dr. Sanders, Father Balthus sat at the organ, his thin fingers drawing from the
pipes their unbroken music, which soared away through
the stained panels of the windows to the distant dismembered sun.

Saraband
for
lepers

For the next three days Sanders remained with Balthus, as the last crystal spurs dissolved from the tissues of his arm. All day he knelt beside the organ, working the foot-bellows with his jeweled arm. As the crystals dissolved, the wound he had torn in his arm ran with blood again, washing the pale prisms of his exposed tissues.

At dusk, when the sun sank in a thousand fragments into the western night, Father Balthus would leave the organ and stand out on the porch, looking up at the spectral trees. His slim scholar's face and calm eyes, their composure belied by the nervous movements of his hands, like the false calm of someone recovering from an attack of fever, would gaze at Sanders as they ate their small supper on a footstool beside the altar, sheltered from the embalming air by the jewels in the cross.

This emblem had been the joint gift of the mining companies, and the immense span of the crosspiece, at least five or six feet, carried its freight of precious stones like the boughs of the crystallized trees in the forest. The rows of emeralds and rubies, between which the smaller diamonds of Mont Royal traced starlike patterns, ran from one end of the crosspiece to the other. The jewels emitted a hard, continuous light so intense that the stones seemed fused together into a cruciform specter.

At first Sanders thought that Balthus regarded his survival as an example of the Almighty's intervention, and made some token expression of gratitude. At this Balthus smiled ambiguously. Why he had returned to the church Sanders could only guess. By now it was surrounded on all sides by the crystal trellises, as if overtopped by the mouth of an immense glacier.

From the door of the chancel Sanders could see the outbuildings of the native school and dormitory that Max Clair had described, presumably the home of the tribe of lepers abandoned by their priest. Sanders mentioned his meeting with the lepers, but Balthus seemed uninterested in his former parishioners or their present fate. Even Sanders's presence barely impinged upon his isolation. Preoccupied with himself, he sat for hours at the organ or wandered among the empty pews.

One morning, however, Balthus found a blind python searching at the door of the porch. Its eyes had been transformed into enormous jewels that rose from its forehead like crowns. Balthus knelt down and picked up the snake, then entwined its long body around his arms. He carried it down the aisle to the altar, and lifted it up to the cross. He watched it with a wry smile when, its sight returned, it slid away among the pews.

On the third day Sanders woke to the early morning light and found Balthus, alone, celebrating the Eucharist. Lying on the pew pulled up to the altar rail, Sanders watched him without moving, but the priest stopped and walked away, stripping off his vestments.

Over breakfast he confided: "You probably wonder what I was doing, but it seemed a convenient moment to test the validity of the sacrament."

He gestured at the prismatic colors pouring through the stained-glass windows. The original scriptural scenes had been transformed into paintings of bewildering abstract beauty, in which the dismembered fragments of the faces of Joseph and Jesus, Mary and the disciples floated on the liquid ultramarine of the refracted sky.

"It may sound heretical to say so, but the body of Christ is with us everywhere here—" he touched the thin shell of crystals on Sanders's arm "in each prism and rainbow, in the ten thousand faces of the sun." He raised his thin hands, jeweled by the light. "So you see, I fear that the Church, like its symbol"—here he pointed to the cross—"may have outlived its function."

Sanders searched for an answer. "I'm sorry. Perhaps if you left here—"

"No!" Balthus insisted, annoyed by Sanders's obtuseness. "Can't you understand? Once I was a true apostate —I knew God existed but could not believe in him." He laughed bitterly at himself. "Now events have overtaken me. For a priest there is no greater crisis, to deny God when he can be seen to exist in every leaf and flower."

With a gesture he led Sanders down the nave to the open porch. He pointed up to the dome-shaped lattice of crystal beams that reached from the rim of the forest like the buttresses of an immense cupola of diamond and glass. Embedded at various points were the almost motionless forms of birds with outstretched wings, golden orioles and scarlet macaws, shedding brilliant pools of light. The bands of color moved through the forest, the reflections of the melting plumage enveloping them in endless concentric patterns. The overlapping arcs hung in the air like the votive windows of a city of cathedrals. Everywhere around them Sanders could see countless smaller birds, butterflies and insects, joining their cruciform haloes to the coronation of the forest.

Father Balthus took Sanders's arm. "In this forest we see the final celebration of the Eucharist of Christ's body. Here everything is transfigured and illuminated, joined together in the last marriage of space and time."

Toward the end, as they stood side by side with their backs to the altar, his conviction seemed to fail him. As the deep frost penetrated the church, the aisle transformed itself into an occluding tunnel of glass pillars. With an expression almost of panic Balthus watched the keys of the organ manual sealing themselves together as they merged into one another, and Sanders knew that he was searching for some means of escape.

Then at last he rallied. He seized the cross from the altar and wrenched it from its stand. With a sudden anger born of absolute conviction he pressed the cross into Sanders's arms. He dragged Sanders to the porch and propelled him to one of the narrowing vaults, through which they could see the distant surface of the river.

"Go! Get away from here! Find the river!"

When Sanders hesitated, trying to control the heavy scepter with his bandaged arm, Balthus shouted fiercely: "Tell them I ordered you to take it!"

Sanders last saw him standing arms outstretched to the approaching walls, in the posture of the illuminated birds, his eyes filled with relief at the first circles of light conjured from his upraised palms.

The crystallization of the forest was now almost complete. Only the jewels in the cross allowed Sanders to make his way through the vaults between the trees. Holding the shaft in his hands, he moved the crosspiece along the trellises that hung everywhere like webs of ice, looking for the weaker panels that would dissolve in the light. As they slid to the ground at his feet he stepped through the openings, pulling the cross with him.

When he reached the river he searched for the bridge he had found when he entered the forest for the second time, but the prismatic surface extended away in a wide bend, its light obliterating the few landmarks he might otherwise have recognized. Above the banks the foliage glowed like painted snow, the only movement coming from the slow traverse of the sun. Here and there a soft blur below the bank revealed itself as the illuminated specter of a lighter or river launch, but nothing else seemed to retain any trace of its previous identity.

Sanders followed the bank, avoiding the faults in the surface and the waist-high needles that grew together on the upper slopes. He came to the mouth of a small stream and began to walk along it, too tired to climb over the cataracts in its path. Although his three days with Father Balthus had rested him sufficiently to realize that some way still remained out of the forest, the absolute silence of the vegetation along the banks and the deep prismatic glow almost convinced him that the entire earth had been transformed and that any progress through this crystal world had become pointless.

At this time, however, he discovered that he was no longer alone in the forest. Whenever the overhead canopy of trees gave way to the open sky, along the bed of the stream or in the small clearings, he passed the half-crystallized bodies of men and women fused against the trunks of the trees, looking up at the refracted sun. Most of them were elderly couples seated together with their bodies fusing into one another as they merged with the trees and the jeweled undergrowth. The only young man he passed was a soldier in field uniform, sitting on a fallen trunk by the edge of the stream. His helmet had blossomed into an immense carapace of crystals, a solar umbrella that enclosed his face and shoulders.

Below the soldier the surface of the stream was traversed by a deep fault. At its bottom a narrow channel of water still flowed, washing the submerged legs of three soldiers who had set out to ford the stream at this point and were now embalmed in its crystal walls. Now and then their legs stirred in a slow liquid way, as if the men, roped together around their waists, were forever marching through this glacier of crystals, their faces lost in the blur of light around them.

There was a distant movement through the forest, and the sound of voices. Sanders hurried on, clasping the heavy cross to his chest. Fifty yards away, in a clearing between two groves of trees, a troupe of people dressed like harlequins were moving through the forest, dancing and shouting to one another. Sanders caught up with them and stopped at the edge of the clearing, trying to count the scores of dark-skinned men and women of all ages, some of them with small children, who were taking part in this graceful saraband. They were wandering in a loose procession, small groups breaking away to dance around single trees or bushes. There were well over a hundred of them, passing through the forest with no evident route in mind. Their arms and faces were transformed by the crystal growth, and already their drab loincloths and robes were beginning to frost and jewel.

As Sanders stood by his cross a small party came over to him in a series of leaps and jumps, then gamboled around him like newly admitted entrants to paradise serenading an attendant archangel. An old man with a deformed light-filled face passed Sanders, gesturing at his fingerless hands as the jeweled light poured from his stunted joints. Sanders remembered the lepers seated beneath the trees near the mission hospital. During the previous days the whole tribe had entered the forest. They danced away from him on their crippled legs, holding their children by the hands, grotesque rainbows dazzling their faces.

As the lepers moved off, Sanders followed behind them, dragging the cross in both hands. Through the trees he saw the train of the procession, but they seemed to vanish as quickly as they appeared, as if eager to familiarize themselves with every tree and grove in their new-found paradise. However, for no reason the entire troupe then turned and came round again, as if delighted to take a last look at Sanders and his cross. As they went by Sanders caught a glimpse of a tall dark-robed woman at their head, calling to the others in a clear voice. Her pale arms and face already shone with the crystal light of the forest. She turned to look back, and Sanders shouted over the bobbing heads: "Suzanne! Suzanne, here—!"

But the woman and the remainder of the troupe had scattered again among the trees. Hobbling along, Sanders found the last remnants of their meager baggage lying on the ground—rag shoes and broken baskets, begging bowls with their few grains of rice already half fused to the vitrified ground.

Once Sanders came across the half-crystallized body of a small child who had fallen behind and been unable to keep up with the others. Lying down to rest, it had become fused to the ground. Sanders listened to the voices fading away among the trees, the child's parents somewhere among them. Then he lowered the cross over the child and waited as the crystals deliquesced from its arms and legs. Freed again, the child's deformed hands clasped the air. With a start it clambered to its feet and ran off through the trees, the dissolving light pouring from its head and shoulders.

Sanders was still following the procession, lost far away in the distance, when he reached the summer house where Thorensen and Serena Ventress had first taken refuge. It was now dusk, and the jewels of the cross shone faintly in the failing light. Already the cross had lost much of its power, and most of the smaller diamonds and rubies had faded to blunted nodes of carbon and corundum. Only the large emeralds still burned strongly against the white hulk of Thorensen's cruiser trapped in its fault in front of the summer house.

Sanders walked along the bank, past the crystal remains of the mulatto in his crocodile skin. The two had become merged, the man himself, half-white and half-black, fusing with the dark jeweled beast. Their own outlines were still visible as they effloresced through each other's tissues. The face of the mulatto shone through the superimposed jaws and eyes of the great crocodile.

The door of the summer house was open. Sanders climbed the steps and walked into the chamber. He looked down at the bed, in whose frosted depths, like swimmers asleep on the bottom of an enchanted pool, Serena and the mine-owner lay together. Thorensen's eyes were closed, and the delicate petals of a blood red rose blossomed from the hole in his breast like an exquisite marine plant. Beside him Serena slept quietly, the unseen motion of her heart sheathing her body in a faint amber glow, the palest residue of life. Although Thorensen had died trying to save her, she lived on in her own half-death.

Something glittered in the dusk behind Sanders. He turned to see a brilliant chimera, a man with incandescent arms and chest, race past among the trees, a cascade of particles diffusing in the air behind him. He flinched back behind the cross, but the man had vanished, whirling himself away among the crystal vaults. As his luminous wake faded Sanders heard his voice echoing across the frosted air, the plaintive words jeweled and ornamented like everything else in that transmogrified world. *"Serena—! Serena—!"*

The
prismatic
sun

Two months later, as he completed his letter to Dr. Paul Derain, director of the leper hospital at Fort Isabelle, in the quiet of his hotel bedroom at Port Matarre, Sanders wrote:

—it seems hard to believe, Paul, here in this empty hotel, that the strange events of that phantasmagoric forest ever occurred. Yet in fact I am little more than forty miles as the crow (or should I say, the gryphon?) flies from the focal area ten miles to the south of Mont Royal, and if I need any reminder there is the barely healed wound on my arm. According to the bartender downstairs—I'm glad to say that he, at least, is still at his post (almost everyone else has left)—the forest is now advancing at the rate of some four hundred yards each day. One of the visiting journalists talking to Louise claims that at this rate of progress at least a third of the earth's surface will be affected by the end of the next decade, and a score of the world's capital cities petrified beneath layers of prismatic crystal, as Miami has already been—no doubt you have seen reports of the abandoned resort as a city of a thousand cathedral spires, a vision materialized from St. John the Divine.

To tell the truth, however, the prospect causes me little worry. As I have said, Paul, it's obvious to me now that its origins are more than physical. When I stumbled out of the forest into an army cordon five miles from Mont Royal, two days after seeing the helpless phantom that had once been Ventress, the gold cross clutched in my arms, I was determined never to visit the forest again. By one of those ludicrous inversions of logic, I found myself, far from acclaimed as a hero, standing summary trial before a military court and charged with looting. The gold cross had apparently been stripped of its jewels—the generous benefaction of the mining companies—and in vain did I protest that these vanished stones had been the price of my survival. Only the intercession of Max Clair and Louise Peret saved me. At our suggestion a patrol of soldiers equipped with jeweled crosses entered the forest in an attempt to find Suzanne and Ventress, but they were forced to retreat.

Whatever my feelings at the time, however, I know now that I shall one day return to the forest at Mont Royal. Each night the fractured disc of the Echo satellite passes overhead, illuminating the midnight sky like a silver chandelier. And I am convinced, Paul, that the sun itself has begun to effloresce. At sunset, when its disc is veiled by the crimson dust, it seems to be crossed by a distinctive latticework, a vast portcullis that will one day spread outwards to the planets and the stars, halting them in their courses.

As the example of that brave apostate priest who gave the cross to me illustrates, there is an immense reward to be found in that frozen forest. There the transfiguration of all living and inanimate forms occurs before our eyes, the gift of immortality a direct consequence of the surrender by each of us of our own physical and temporal identities. However apostate we may be in this world, there perforce we become apostles of the prismatic sun.

So when my recovery is complete I shall return to Mont Royal with one of the scientific expeditions passing through here. It should not be too difficult to arrange my escape and then I shall return to the solitary church in that enchanted world, where by day fantastic birds fly through the petrified forest and jeweled crocodiles glitter like heraldic salamanders on the banks of the crystalline rivers, and where by night the illuminated man races among the trees, his arms like golden cartwheels and his head like a spectral crown.

Putting down his pen as Louise Peret entered the room, Dr. Sanders folded the letter and placed it in an old envelope from Derain in which he had written asking for Sanders's plans.

Louise came over to the desk by the window and put her hand on Sanders's shoulder. She wore a clean white dress that emphasized the drabness of the rest of Port Matarre—despite the transformation of the forest only a few miles away, here at the mouth of the river the vegetation still retained its somber appearance, although the motes of light that flickered within the foliage marked the crystallization soon to come.

"Are you still writing to Derain?" she asked. "It's a long letter."

"There's a lot to say." Sanders sat back, clasping her hand as he looked out at the deserted arcade below. A few military landing craft were moored against the police jetty, and beyond them the dark river swept away into the interior. The main military base was now at one of the large government plantations ten miles up-river. Here an airfield had been constructed and the many hundreds of scientists and technicians, not to mention journalists, still trying to gain some understanding of the advancing forest were flown in directly, so by-passing Port Matarre. Once again the riverside town was half deserted. The native market had closed down. The stall holders with their crystallized ornaments had been put out of business by the forest's own over-abundant economy. However, now and then, during his walks around Port Matarre, Sanders would see some solitary mendicant hanging around near the barracks or police prefecture, an old blanket in his basket hiding some grotesque offering of the forest—a crystallized parrot or river-carp, and once, the head and thorax of a baby.

"Are you resigning then?" Louise asked. "I think you should reconsider—we've talked—"

"My dear, one can't reconsider things to a hundred places of decimals. Somewhere one's got to make a decision." Sanders took the letter from his pocket and tossed it on to the desk. Not to hurt Louise, who had stayed with him in the hotel since his rescue, he said: "Actually, I haven't made up my mind yet. I'm just using the letter to work the whole thing out."

Louise nodded, looking down at him. Sanders noticed that she had begun to wear her sunglasses again, unconsciously revealing her own private decision about Sanders and his future, and their own inevitable separation. However, minor dishonesties such as this were merely the price of their own tolerance of one another.

"Have the police any news about Anderson?" Sanders

asked. During their first month in Port Matarre Louise had gone down to the prefecture every morning in the hope of getting some news about her lost colleague, partly, Sanders guessed, to justify her extended stay with him in the hotel. That she could now dispense with this small squaring of her conscience meant that she had made other arrangements. "They might have heard something—you never know. You haven't been down?"

"No. Hardly anyone is entering the zone now." Louise shrugged. "I suppose it's worth trying."

"Of course." Sanders stood up, leaning on the injured arm, and then put on his jacket.

"How is it?" Louise asked. "Your arm. It seems all right now."

Sanders patted the elbow. "I think it's healed. Louise, it's been good of you to look after me. You know that."

Louise regarded him from behind her sunglasses. A brief smile, not without affection, touched her lips. "What more could I do?" She laughed at this, and then strolled to the door. "I must go up to my room and change. Enjoy your walk."

Sanders followed her to the door, and then held her arm for a moment. When she had gone he stood by the door, listening to the few sounds in the almost empty hotel.

Sitting down at the desk again, he read through his letter to Paul Derain. Thinking about Louise at the same time, he realized that he could hardly blame her for deciding to leave him. Sanders had in fact forced her out, not so much by his behavior at Port Matarre but simply by not being wholly there—his real identity still moved through the forests of Mont Royal. During his journey down-river in the ambulance craft with Louise and Max Clair, and his subsequent convalescence at Port Matarre, he had felt like the empty projection of a self that still wandered through the forest with the jeweled cross in his arms, re-animating the lost children he passed like a deity on his day of creation. Louise knew nothing of this, and assumed that he was searching for Suzanne.

There was a knock on the door, and Max Clair let himself into the room. Greeting Sanders with a wave, he put his surgical bag down on a chair. Since his arrival in Port Matarre he had been helping at the clinic run by the Jesuit fathers. On several occasions the latter had made an attempt to see Sanders, for the purpose, he guessed, of questioning him about Father Balthus's self-immolation within the forest. Obviously they suspected that his real concern had not been for his parish.

"Morning to you, Edward—I hope I'm not disturbing your meditation for the day?"

"I've finished." When Max glanced toward the half-open door of the bathroom Sanders said: "Louise is upstairs. Now, what's the news today?"

"No idea—I haven't got time to hang around the police station. We're much too busy at the clinic. They're coming in from every hedge and byway."

"What do you expect—there's a doctor there now." Sanders shook his head. "Bring a doctor into a place like Port Matarre and you immediately create a major health problem."

"Well—" Max glanced at Sanders over his glasses, unsure how serious he was being. "I don't know about that. We certainly are busy, Edward. As a matter of fact, now that your arm is better we thought—the fathers, principally—that you might come and give us a hand. Just a couple of mornings a week to start with. The fathers would be grateful to you."

"I dare say." Sanders looked out at the distant forest. "I'd like to help you, Max, of course. As it happens, I'm rather busy at present."

"But you're not. You're just sitting here all day. Look, it's routine largely, nothing to take your mind off higher things, a few maternity cases, pellagra." He added quietly: "Yesterday a couple of cases of leprosy came in—I thought you might be interested."

Sanders turned and studied Max's face, with its bright shortsighted eyes below the domed head. The element of guile, if any, in this last remark was hard to assess. For some time Sanders had suspected that Max had known all along that Suzanne would run away into the forest after seeing Sanders, and that his own pointless search among the hill settlements had been a deliberate means of making sure that no one stopped her. During their time in Port Matarre Max rarely referred to Suzanne, although his wife by now would be frozen like an icon somewhere within the crystal forest. Yet Max's last reference to the lepers, unless intended to provoke him into returning to the forest suggested that in fact Max had no idea of the significance of the forest for Suzanne and Sanders, that for both of them the only final resolution of the imbalance within their minds, their inclination toward the dark side of the equinox, could be found within that crystal world.

"Two cases of leprosy? I'm not interested in the least." Before Max could speak Sanders went on: "Frankly, Max, I'm not sure whether I'm still qualified to help you."

"What? Of course you are."

"In absolute terms. It seems to me, Max, that the whole profession of medicine may have been superseded. —I don't think the simple distinction between life and death has much meaning now. Rather than try to cure those patients you should put them into a launch and send them up-river to Mont Royal."

Max stood up. He made a gesture of helplessness, and then said cheerfully: "I'll come back tomorrow. Keep an eye on yourself."

When he had gone Sanders completed his letter, adding a final paragraph and farewell. Sealing it into a fresh envelope, he addressed it to Derain and propped it against the inkwell. He then took out his checkbook and signed one of the checks. He slipped these into a second envelope on which he wrote Louise's name.

As he stood up, buttoning his jacket, he noticed Louise and Max talking in the street outside the hotel. Recently he had often seen them together, in the foyer of the hotel or at the door of the restaurant. He waited until their conversation ended and then went down to the foyer.

At the desk he paid the previous week's bills for himself and Louise, and settled their accounts for a further fortnight. After exchanging a few pleasantries with the Portuguese owner, Sanders went out for his usual pre-lunch stroll.

Usually his walk took him down to the river. He strolled through the deserted arcades, noticing, as he did each morning, the strange contrasts between light and shadow despite the apparent absence of direct sunlight in Port Matarre. At the corner, opposite the police prefecture, he flexed his injured arm for the last time against one of the pillars. Somewhere in the crystalline streets of Mont Royal were the missing fragments of himself, living on in their own prismatic medium.

Thinking of Captain Radek and of Suzanne Clair, Sanders reached the waterfront and walked down along the deserted jetties. Almost all the native boats had gone, and the settlements on the other side of the river had been abandoned.

One craft, however, as usual still patrolled the empty waterfront. Three hundred yards away Sanders could see the red-and-yellow speedboat in which he and Louise had first made their journey to Mont Royal. The tall figure of Aragon stood at the helm, letting the boat drift on the tide. Every morning he would watch Sanders walk by, but the two men never spoke to one another.

Sanders walked toward him, feeling the wallet in his jacket. As he reached Aragon the latter waved to him, then started his motor and moved off. Puzzled by this, Sanders walked on, and then saw that Aragon was taking the craft down-river to the point of the bank where the crystallized body of Matthieu had been cast up two months earlier.

Sanders caught up with the boat, and then walked

down the bank toward it. For a moment the two men regarded each other.

"A fine boat you have there, Captain," Sanders said at last, repeating the phrase he had first used to Aragon.

Half an hour later, as they moved off up-river, Sanders leaned back in his seat when they passed the central wharves. In the choppy water the spray broke unevenly, the fallen rainbows carried away in the dark wake behind them. In the street between the arcades an old Negro was standing in the dust with a white shield in his hand, waiting for the boat to go past. On the police jetty Louise Peret stood next to Max Clair. Her eyes hidden by the sunglasses, she watched Sanders without waving as the boat sped on up the deserted river.

Printed in the USA
CPSIA information can be obtained
at www.ICGtesting.com
LVHW091132150724
785511LV00001B/103